FACE OFF

A WAR, THAT NEVER ENDS.

RAJAN JHA

GIRJE PUBLISHER
*Creative   *Innovative   *Extensive

Published by
Girje Publisher
5/5, Awantipura,
Opp. Jivajiganj Police Station,
Ujjain - 456006, Madhya Pradesh, India.
www.girjepublisher.com

ISBN: 978-81-937915-1-6

eBook: 978-81-937915-0-9

The moral right of the author has been asserted.

Cover Design by **Amit Girje**

Editing & Proofreading by **Stéphanie Indurain**

Cover Illustration Copyright © 2018 by Girje Publisher

Book Design and Production by www.girjepublisher.com

Powered by AG Technologies USA, LLC - www.agtechnologiesusa.com

---

Content Disclaimer

This is a fictitious work; the story may contain some offensive words. To protect the privacy of certain individuals the names, identifying details and some places names have been changed. Cigarette and alcohol are injurious to health; Publisher and Author neither support nor recommend it in any way.

To Maa, Papa and my Dear Diksha.

Acknowledgments

Many people influenced me to write this book. I would like to thank all of them.

Firstly, the great Indian Armed Forces; who have protected us since Independence.

A special thanks to Mr. Yogendra Dubey; Sir, you know the reason.

Shrutiman Shukla, Rahul Chandra Jha, Prayashi Bhardwaj, Sumeet Raj, and Mohit Shrivastava; for giving me the motivation, every day to complete the book.

I am thankful to Mr. Uday and Mrs. Satrupa for continuously 'torturing' me to finish the book.

Paramvir Singh Randhava and Abhishek Katoch for no reason; it's just both of you are lucky that I am with you.

Thanks to Girje Publisher for allowing me to get my name in the ocean of print media.

At last, Alam sir... someday...

Hang on; before you begin this book, you need to answer some questions.

- What do you think about the Army?
- Is the job of a soldier easy?
- Can you imagine a country without the army?
- Do media and politicians disclose the real problems of the military in front of the citizens?
- Do soldiers make fun and friendship with the enemy standing in front of them?
- Can your enemy be your friend for a while?
- Why is "Made in China" almost everywhere in the world?

Be honest, ask these questions of yourself.

Wait, have you done the task? Have you got the answers to the questions?

Be honest, think twice and ask yourself again.

If not, let's begin the story, and you will get all the answers.

The author is a traveler and nature photographer. He has a keen interest in music and mythology. The idea of the book came after Sikkim's visit.

Rajan Jha was born in Madhubani, Bihar, India. He studied in Jhabua and Dhar district, in Madhya Pradesh state.

"This is not just a book; it is the story of every soldier's life."

This story is about a soldier, military life, friendship with the enemy, love, family, feelings, and of course, a war that never ends...

'Hi,' Prashant extended his hand across the barbed wire. There was a broad smile on his face. A welcoming face, maybe his face was not so welcoming because the last time he shaved was six days ago and his beard has grown back. But his gesture was a sign of friendship. After looking for a few minutes into each other's eyes, a hand suddenly appeared along with a smile.

'Hi, I am captain Wang,' said the guy on the other side of the fence. His smile was suspicious, but a broad forehead and a pair of spectacles gave the impression of a great intellectual.

'And you?' Captain Wang asked.

'I am Captain Kabir,' Prashant replied with hesitation; 'yes, you may call me Kabir.'

'So, how are you?' Prashant asked.

'I am good and what about you?' Wang replied.

'Do you understand English?' Prashant enquired. As he had met many of these officers, but most of them know a little or no English. Therefore, he avoided interacting with these officers.

'Yes, I do,' Wang replied with a smile.

That was so nice as finally, he had met someone with whom he could at least interact, at least he could try to learn what was in their heart. Suddenly he wanted to talk about a thousand things. It seemed as if he was waiting for one guy to share, to understand. He had thousands of questions in his mind. He started selecting and prioritizing. After a few seconds of silence, Prashant asked: 'how do you speak English so well?'

'In China, English is taught in school,' Wang replied.

'But the other officers do not speak very much, why's that?' Prashant could not stop himself from asking the question.

'Maybe because they were not interested at school,' Wang said.

'And you?' Prashant asked.

'I love learning languages and new things,' Wang replied.

'So, have you done a Ph.D. or something?'

'No, actually this was one of the subjects at my university.'

'Wow, I thought that in China English was forbidden.'

'No it's not, after university, I learned to speak English, and then I followed a course in Beijing to become an interpreter.'

'Oh! That's so nice, now I think I could learn to speak Chinese; will you teach me?'

There was a sudden silence in the air. Prashant had asked his enemy to teach him the language. Even the person on duty gave them a strange look.

'Will you teach me Hindi?' Wang broke the silence.

They shook hands. Prashant wanted to hug him, they were both comfortable, and they had forgotten that they were enemies.

'Do you know we like Hindi movies?' Wang continued.

'Really, don't say that today, said Prashant, you are changing my thought process.'

'Not all movies are screened, but I guess all the big hits are screened in China nowadays.'

'How many have you watched so far?'

'I don't remember them all, but there was a movie that I have watched recently Wand said as he recalled something.

'Which one?' Prashant asked.

'I don't remember its name, but the story is about Kushti,' Wang said.

'Yes, there are two movies 'Dangal' and 'Sultan.'

'I don't remember its name.'

'What's the story then I may help?'

'It's about a father teaching his daughter Kushti.'

'Oh! It's Dangal, it's a nice movie, top-rated in India,' Prashant replied.

'Yes, I guess it's Dangal.' Wang nodded.

'And what about the second one, do you remember?' The curiosity was increasing.'

'It's a little old,' Wang replied.

'I guess it's not 'Raja Harishchandra' or 'Devdas.' Prashant commented.

'What?' Wang asked. He was bewildered. He had never heard in his life heard the names of these movies.

'Relax just joking, if you tell me the story, I will help you to find the name,' Prashant replied.

'It's about three friends in college; they are searching for one of their friends,' Wang said.

'Three Idiots,' Prashant said.

'I guess so; with a look of strain on his face he replied: 'Yeah, it's three idiots.'

'Wow, I thought you people didn't watch Indian movies,' Prashant said.

'Do you watch Chinese movies?' Wang asked.

This was his first question apart from the introduction, and this question made Prashant feel sympathetic about himself. He felt embarrassed, but with a fake smile he replied: 'yes, why would we not watch them?'

'Which one?' Wang asked.

'Ah! Actually, I don't remember its name.'

'Not an issue you can tell the story.'

Now Wang was to play 'Dumb Charades.'

After thinking for a while, Prashant replied: 'it's about a girl whose father leaves her at childhood, and she tries to find him but she fails, and then after so many years she finds him and takes him back to their home. It's a happy ending, do you remember?' The story was fake; he had never watched any Chinese movie, but his confidence made Wang think.

After thinking for some time, Wang replied: 'I don't remember the movie.'

'Maybe you have not watched it, but it's a very nice movie, and you should watch it,' Prashant replied with a sigh of relief.

'So, what else?' Wang asked.

'Nothing much.'

The soft wind started to touch their cheeks. Prashant began to look towards the far end of the Chinese territory. The clouds had started mustering in the remote valley. After five days of continuous drizzle, it was a bright day. This was one of the reasons Prashant had come out of his tent. Since the morning he had not gone back to his tent. Duties were rotated and also, he was called for breakfast several times, but after consecutive gloomy days and nights, it was even worth skipping one odd meal. He kept on sitting and enjoying the dose of vitamin D.

'What a beautiful view,' said Prashant looking admiringly at the clouds.

Wang looked towards him, but then he too turned his attention towards the other direction and nodded.

'Are those clouds Chinese?' Prashant asked in a satirical tone.

'Yeah, right now they are Chinese,' Wang replied in affirmation.

'But after some time, they will come to India?'

'Then it will be a gift from us,' Wang prompted.

'That's the problem with you people,' Prashant looked at Wang with a hardened voice.

'Relax man, I was just kidding,' Wang replied.

A smile returned to Prashant's face, and he said: 'how can someone define the boundaries of river, wind, sunlight?'

'You seem to be philosophical. Are you interested in philosophy?' Wang asked.

'No, no, it's just random thoughts. I don't read or follow a certain philosophy,' Prashant said.

'Hey if you don't mind, can I ask you something?' Prashant asked, after a silence of several minutes, Prashant asked.

'Yes; why not?'

'What do you think about Dalai Lama?' Prashant asked.

'What do you mean?' Wang said.

Prashant was expecting the question but not in a soft tone. Wang replied calmly. Prashant did not want to escalate but couldn't help asking.

'I mean like in India, he is considered as a religious preacher.'

'Not in China. He is a separatist,' Wang answered.

'But as far as I know, the PLA invaded Tibet,' Now, Prashant was expecting a shut-up call.

But Wang replied: 'PLA liberated Tibet.'

'What do you mean?' Prashant felt amazed because it was the first time he heard something like that.

'I will explain to you. Actually, there was a slavery system in Tibet, and Dalai Lama wanted to become king. Therefore, help was asked for by the Tibetans and PLA liberated them.'

'But many Tibetan people I have seen in the news keep protesting against China, who are they then?' Prashant enquired.

'They are just a small percentage. Moreover, you know approximately 90% of Tibetans live in Beijing and other major provinces and enjoy their lives.'

'Is it? I thought there was an important problem in Tibet.'

'But where do you see all these things?' Wang enquired.

'In the media,' Prashant replied.

'Your media shows anything I guess,' Wang commented.

'Yes, that's true, but our media is an independent media, unlike yours.'

'No, it's not like that, our media is a sensible media.'

'Your media is just a spokesperson,' Prashant commented.

'No, our media is sensible, unlike your media which is showing anything about the standoff,' Wang replied.

'Leave this topic, now just reply to one question. Can your media blame your government or your prime minister for anything?'

'What do you mean?' Wang asked.

'I give you an example. I hope you know Kashmir.'

'I know, it's a disputed area between India and Pakistan.'

'Yes, now Indian media freely blames the army, the government, the home minister and even the prime minister for its internal issues. There are debates, articles and many things. And do you know what, they are still alive? Unlike yours where student protestors were wiped out,' Prashant said.

Wang kept silent for a few seconds, he seemed to be choking, but after gulping, he replied: 'even China has many problems, and it's true, but things do not pop up in the media so easily.'

'What sort of problem?' Prashant interfered.

'Like you have Kashmir and terrorism, it's also there in China.'

'What?' Prashant shocked.

'Yes, even China faces terrorism, now it's a great concern. Even separatist movements have strengthened their voices. These are serious problems, but our government is handling them well.' Wang summarized and repeated: 'The government is handling them well,' there was not much satisfaction in his answer though.

Prashant sensing his discomfort changed the topic 'hey leave it. What do you think about India and Indians? As a civilian, I mean.'

'Whenever we hear about India, we imagine rivers, mountains, temples, mosques, colors. I know India is a diverse and beautiful country. In fact, what do they say ahh... incredible, yes incredible India?' Wang said.

A broad smile returned to each man's face.

'And what do you people think about China?' Wang questioned.

'Cell phones: Vivo/Oppo, noodles,' Prashant replied.

They both laughed loudly. There seemed to be no tension at all. Troops from both sides were amazed seeing both of them talking.

Somebody has correctly said we all are human beings, and so are friends unless a rusty smelling bullet leaves the muzzle.

'So, are you Buddhist?' Prashant asked. Prashant was not able to understand why was he acting like an interviewer? Many questions he had already ignored and filtered thousands of times before asking. He wanted to learn through experience. He never believed in reading much because his philosophy was that only individual can truly talk about himself, not a third person, therefore, why he should learn from Americans about China. For Prashant, Wang was the authority that day, and whatsoever knowledge he would gain, he would believe in it.

'No,' Wang replied.

'Then?'

'Then what?' Wang asked.

'You must be Christian?' Prashant guessed.

'No, I am not Christian,' Wang said.

'Then what are you?' Prashant questioned curiously.

'Well, I don't have any religion,' Wang answered calmly after taking a deep breath.

'How is it possible?' Prashant was shocked.

'What?' Prashant enquired.

'No, I mean I have heard that China is a Buddhist nation and if you are not Buddhist then you must be Christian because Christianity was sold and traded during the colonial period,' Prashant questioned.

'No, not every Chinese is Buddhist,' Wang confirmed.

'Really,' Prashant said.

'Yes, actually many people do not follow any religion in China,' Wang said.

'But your mother and father must have some religion?' Prashant could not stop himself.

'No, they also don't have any religion, but my mother follows the preaching of Buddha, but Buddhism does not dominate us,' Wang said.

'You know, it's complicated for me to accept it mentally? Because in India everybody belongs to a religion,' Prashant said.

'So, what is your religion?' Wang asked the same question.

'Hindu, when I was born, but now I also don't follow any religion,' Prashant said.

'Why?' Wang was confused.

'Now, I am a soldier, and a soldier does not have any religion. I have only one god, and that's my flag,' Prashant replied with pride.

Wang nodded in affirmation. They both looked at the flag which was not too far. The wind was blowing both their flags high with pride.

'Have you eaten?' Prashant asked.

'Yes,' Wang replied.

'When? It's 13:30 now, and I guess it's lunchtime,' Prashant enquired.

'It's 13:30 in India, not in China. In China, it's 15:30,' Wang confirmed.

'Oh sorry, I forgot. So, what did you have for lunch?' Prashant asked.

'Rice, beef, and soup, in any meal you add soup it will become typical Chinese food,' Wang said.

'Oh… that's great, I'm starving, I should go and eat. I guess my senior officers are waiting,' Prashant said as he hurried away.

'Ok then, see you,' Wang replied.

After shaking hands, Prashant went to his tent for lunch. Everyone giggled when Prashant shared his exchange with Wang.

'Ram Sahab,' somebody called from outside the tent.

'Yes, who's there?' Prashant asked putting a chapatti onto his plate.

'Sahib, this is Raghu, there is something urgent.'

'Now what; can I not at least, have my meal in peace? Can't these Chinese sit and enjoy this weather?' Prashant cursing the Chinese put his plate aside and went out of the tent asking 'what is it now?'

'Sahib, look over there, they are building something.'

Prashant looked in the direction that Raghu was pointing. He felt disappointed. It was the same place where just a few minutes ago Prashant and Wang had had an exciting and friendly conversation.

'Son of a bitch,' Prashant cursed at the top of his voice. Everybody came out of the tent.

'Hi… at least let me have my meal,' Prashant controlling his anger and with a smile on his face complained to Wang.

Wang didn't reply. He whispered something to the person standing next to him. After looking sharply towards Prashant, the man said something in Chinese to Wang.

'My colonel says that he will only talk to somebody of equal rank,' Wang told Prashant in a soft voice.

'I will pass on the message. But at least stop right now Wang,' Prashant said with hope.

'I can't. I am just an interpreter,' Wang whispered.

Wang walked towards the colonel and conveyed Prashant's reply. The Chinese colonel said something in Chinese angrily. The five soldiers started digging as fast as they could.

Wang and Prashant looked at each other. Prashant could see the disappointment in Wang's eyes. The men were only following the orders. The weather has started picking up. The brightly shining sun was displaying its last few rays. Soon they too got covered by the thick black clouds. The day turned into night suddenly across the plateau. Prashant and Wang were still looking at each other. The barbed wire was still standing, separating five meters into an infinite distance.

'**P**rashant turn off the alarm,' Mohit shouted without even taking his head out of his sleeping bag.

It was really annoying waking up at 05:00 in a place where without even looking out of tent one could imagine that the night was freezing, and yet one can also find beautiful ice patches on the outside of their tent. Moreover, it was Sunday, and after last night's extra beer, a lie in was called for. Apart from the almighty sun, which has a boring routine every day, nobody was willing to leave their bed. It was a different thing when everyone was awake because of soldierly habit, but nobody was ready to open their eyes.

'Good morning sir,' Prashant said, switching off the alarm.

'F*ck your morning, what's so good about this morning? At least today you could have changed the timing; it's Sunday OK. After a hard month, we got today's Sunday, and your alarm has ruined that as well,' Mohit was now wide awake, but he was not ready to get up.

Prashant and Mohit shared a tent, and they had been sharing in earlier exercises as well. Though Mohit was senior to Prashant, they shared a very healthy relationship. Since the day Prashant reported to the unit, Mohit had always taken his care as his younger brother and did justice as his subordinate. Prashant had also, never ever crossed the limit apart from making fun of his subordinate sometimes, but Mohit had never minded. He was very comfortable with it.

'Sir, I am sorry, but wake up, look outside what a beautiful morning it is.' Prashant repeated putting on his jacket and moving out of the tent: 'Sir, please come and see.'

'Hi Prashant,' said Vikas.

'Good morning Sir, you are awake early,' Prashant said.

'Yes, I am, and it's stunning today.'

'Sir, not even beer could make you remain asleep in the morning. How can you wake up so early every morning? Please give me some tips; otherwise, I will be paying a fine for not attending PT at our peace location.' Prashant said smilingly in the way of complaint.

'I don't know, it's from childhood that I wake up early, but not today. In fact, today your annoying alarm made me get out of bed. Can you please call someone for a chair and a cup of tea? Let's sit and watch the view.'

'Roger Sir.'

Vikas and Uday shared a tent just next to Prashant's tent. Though Vikas was the most senior officer with them, all his junior subordinates were very comfortable with him.

There was the sound of sipping of tea at 15000ft. The day was beautiful; they were both continuously praising nature and its beauty. The sun had shown its face after three days of rain, and its rays had unfolded the beautiful flowers, and there was a great light from the top of the mountains which were just opposite them. The ice, so beautifully placed that it looked like a cup cone with white ice cream. The small birds were chirruping together. There was even a high current in the stream flowing down. The dispersed loose soil and stones looked well placed. It seemed that these entire three days God was painting something above the raining clouds and finally when he was satisfied, he just uncovered his painting for the humans to see.

'A thing of beauty is a joy forever, its loveliness increases; it never goes into nothingness,' Prashant murmured looking at the far end.

'What?' Vikas asked, looking at him.

'This is a poem of John Keats,' Prashant said.

'So?' Vikas asked.

'Today I realize its true meaning. Haven't you heard of him?' Prashant asked.

'No, I don't think so,' Vikas tried to recall.

'Sir, do you know he died when he was in his late twenties? But he is considered one of the best romantic poets. He is even compared with William Wordsworth,' Prashant explained.

'Really,' Vikas asked, and said: 'I was not aware.'

'Actually sir, he was in the hospital due to hereditary cancer or some other disease; I don't remember. Actually, he fell in love with a nurse but he was heartbroken and then his love turned towards nature. His writings were published after his death. This I learned in the eleventh grade, and I could never forget these two lines of his poem sir. Really, sir, nature is beautiful every moment, every day.'

'Yeah, that's true. I will definitely read this poem.'

'Good morning sir, has he started talking about poetry again?' Mohit said as he took his chair out.

'Oh! Hi, Good morning Mohit. Come and sit down. Prashant, can you please call for some tea for Mohit?' Vikas said as he shifted his chair to make some space for Mohit.

'Roger Sir,' replied Prashant.

'Prashant was enlightening me about this beautiful nature. Apart from the military, he knows many things,' Mohit said.

Before Vikas could say anything, Prashant said, 'the military is my job, so definitely I will learn everything gradually, but I have a philosophy in life.'

'See he is a philosopher also,' Mohit intervened.

'Let him speak,' Vikas said: 'so what were you saying?'

'Sir we must have some talent, some hobbies, otherwise, these few colors of the military will ruin us.'

'Wow, what a philosophy,' Uday said satirically.

'Good morning sir.' Uday was a senior subordinate of Mohit.

'Come Uday, have a seat. Yaar, Prashant, ask for one more cup please,' Vikas said.

'Roger Sir.'

'Sir really apart from military he loves everything. That's so nice, at least I am getting to know about you all,' Vikas said.

Mohit and Prashant had been commissioned after Vikas left for out posting. Coming back after five years he was delighted knowing his junior subordinates. He was of Uday's age when he left and returned as the senior officer. He could only become senior as per his service, but his heart was still that of a lieutenant. Vikas had met Prashant just one month ago when everybody was preparing for induction in a training area. During the exercises, everybody was busy with the given tasks and training and now, since it was a Sunday and training was over, Vikas could learn out about Prashant and his interests.

'So, he is interested in philosophy,' Vikas asked.

'Sometimes he writes some shit too,' Mohit said.

'Wow, now he is a writer as well.'

'Sometimes sir...ah... I will check on the tea,' Prashant was feeling embarrassed and moved towards tea point tent.

'He is a good chap I guess.'

'He is very talented sir. I don't know why he is in the army? He would have done very well in the civilian world.' Mohit said, looking towards Prashant, who was at a distance; and couldn't hear Mohit's voice.

'Really sir, he is very talented,' Uday added.

'Ok let's see,' Vikas said, shaking his head in affirmation. 'Light up Uday.'

'Oh, sorry sir,' Uday took a cigarette out and lit up. All three shared the cigarette.

'I don't know why they put such a dirty and ugly picture on the cigarette box?' Vikas said looking at the box.

The air warmed with the cigarette smoke, and all three started looking towards the candy mountain.

'The things of beauty, a joy forever...' Vikas murmured.

'Sahib, there is a phone call for you,' Gautam said.

'Who is it?' Vikas asked.

'The phone exchange says it's the Commanding officer.'

'The Commanding officer,' all three spoke at the same time.

'At 06:30, why does the Commanding officer wants to talk to you?' Uday asked.

'How would I know? Let me go and see, I can't think of any reason for calling so early.' Vikas left his chair and went to answer the phone, which was kept in his tent.

'Sir, where is Vikas?' Prashant asked.

'Your friend has called,' Mohit said.

'The Commanding officer at this time but why?' Prashant asked in confusion.

'Let Vikas sir tell us,' Uday said.

'Here Vikas sir is coming back,' said Mohit looking at Vikas, Everybody got up from their chairs.

'Settle down gentlemen,' said Vikas, taking his chair.

'What has happened sir?' Prashant asked.

'There are a few instructions,' Vikas said in a heavy tone and with a severe gesture.

'Now what, can't he sleep peacefully? He has ruined our month already. At least he should enjoy Sunday,' Uday growled, jumping up from his chair.

'Really Sunday should be a day off. At least now, when exercise is over,' Mohit added.

'Calm down, he is our commanding officer, and we have to follow his orders,' Vikas advised in the same tone.

'That's what we have been doing from the very first day. We are just dancing to his tune,' Mohit said turning his head to the other side.

'Guys, listen: It's serious,' Vikas said.

When Vikas had everyone's attention, he said: 'he has asked me whether he has not disturbed me in my sleep. So, I said no, after that he said if everyone is sleeping then let them sleep and once they all wake up, plan for a picnic, where we all can go and enjoy ourselves.'

'What, a picnic?' Uday shouted, his mouth open wide.

'Yes, a picnic and he has distributed responsibilities,' Vikas confirmed.

'Mohit you will choose the picnic spot, Uday you will detail the vehicle, and Prashant you will cater for food and some drinks. Pass this message to the canteen staff to prepare accordingly,' Vikas ordered.

'Really sir,' Prashant asked as he could not believe his ears.

'Arrange it fast. Don't stare at me like that,' Vikas said.

'Roger Sir,' all three answered unanimously: 'Jai Hind Sir' and all three went to their tasks.

Vikas went to his tent, picked up his intercom and called, 'Vikas for SM, tell the boys to pack up. Today there will be a picnic and tomorrow induction. The vehicle will be detailed later on.'

The whole camp was looking tired after exhaustive drills and practices for one month, they were taking a rest. When Vikas's message circulated, everyone felt like they had an energetic fire burning inside them. A sudden flow of energy spread throughout the camp area.

'Sir, I have selected a place,' Uday came after one hour and said.

'Yes, which one,' Vikas asked.

'Sir, there is a hot spring just twenty-five minutes away from here,' Uday replied.

'That's excellent. Today, the weather is also clear, and the hot spring will be the best option. I will inform the Commanding officer.' Picking up his intercom, he dialed the number of the Commanding officer.

'Jai Hind Sir,' Vikas speaking.'

'Jai Hind Vikas,' The CO said on the other end of the intercom.

'Sir, we have planned to go to a hot spring,' Vikas informed him.

'That's excellent, let's meet at 0900hr after having breakfast. We will have lunch there, and at 1600hr we will return.'

'Roger Sir.'

The intercom disconnected, and the instructions were given by Vikas and everybody started preparing. All three officers gathered at 0800hr in Vikas's tent.

'Have you told the kitchen about breakfast?' Vikas asked.

'It must be coming sir, I told them half an hour ago,' Prashant affirmed taking the chair and settling himself.

'It will be great fun, won't it sir?' Mohit asked.

'Definitely sir, at 15000 ft putting our legs in a hot spring, watching the sky so close, I am getting really excited,' Uday said.

'Yes... really, it will be great fun, and a break like this is required. I don't know why you people keep on cursing your Commanding officer?'

'Sir, this is the first time he has thought of such a picnic; otherwise, he is just a workaholic, everyone knows. Ask Mohit if you don't believe me,' Uday said while unwrapping the candy.

'Really sir, when we have inducted, you will see. He comes to the office at 0830hr sharp and then leaves at 1500hr. At 1600hr, he comes for games and then sits in the office till 2300hr. We get frustrated,' Mohit said in defense of Uday.

'Sir, he is married, and we are bachelors. At least he should think about people like us,' Prashant added.

'Yes, that's a valid point Prashant. I will definitely convey this point to our beloved CO,' said Vikas as he lit his cigarette.

'Prashant, are you taking your guitar to the picnic?' Uday asked.

'Yes sir, I have already told you, it will be there sir,' Prashant said.

'Wait... Wait... Who plays the guitar? Now, don't say it's Prashant,' Vikas asked, he was amazed.

'Sir…. I can play a little,' Prashant replied, not wanting to draw attention to himself.: 'Sir, breakfast is here, should we start?'

'Please, my writer, philosopher and now a musician as well,' Vikas said exhaling the cigarette smoke: 'how many more shades do you have?'

'Sir, we should call him Fifty Shades of Prashant,' Mohit added.

'Yes, that's true, Fifty Shades of Prashant,' Uday clapped, and all three laughed.

'Tring… Tring…' The phone rang.

'Jai Hind, Major Vikas here.'

'Jai Hind Sir, The CO wants to talk to you,' the man on the other end of intercom said.

'Ok,' Vikas answered.

'Jai Hind Sir, Vikas speaking.'

'Ok… Vikas, there is a little change in the plans. I want all company commanders and platoon commanders in the Ops room in the next ten minutes,' the CO said.

'Roger Sir,' Vikas replied.

Vikas put the receiver down and turned towards all of them and said: 'Ops room in next ten minutes.'

'What, but why?' Uday asked.

'I don't know, ask your platoon commanders to be there,' Vikas ordered.

'Roger Sir,' all three said, and off they went.

The Ops room was activated in five minutes, and within ten minutes everyone had settled down. Curiosity was written on everyone's face. Nobody was aware of what had happened?

'Steady up. Jai Hind Sir, all in,' Vikas saluted and gave the report to the commanding officer.

'At ease everyone; Vikas, take your seat,' The CO said as he came inside.

He sat on his chair which was placed in the center of the room. A table covered with a combat cloth was set as usual. The ops room was about to be dismantled, but then suddenly, the soldier in charge received orders for a conference. He had just removed the camouflage from top of the tent, the moment he received orders for the conference, he placed the chairs and sand map back in the same place, as quickly as possible.

The CO picked up the glass of water which had already been placed on the table. He sipped and put it down again, and looked around. Everyone was staring at him in curiosity

'I have received a phone call from Headquarters. In the next three hours, we have to pack up everything and get prepared to march. Picnic over,' he said, he got up and started marching out.

'Steady up, Jai Hind Sir, May I have the permission to break off?' Vikas asked as he stood up.

The CO waved his hand and went out.

'At ease everyone,' Vikas commanded.

The moment Vikas gave the command at ease, everyone started talking about this new and impromptu task. There was suddenly great chaos.

'Relax everyone, keep quiet' Vikas said. But his voice remained unheard as the intensity of questions increased.

'Shut up,' Vikas shouted at the top of his voice. 'Shut up.' The whole ops room fell silent. 'Even I don't know anything, stop wasting time, just do as ordered. Everyone break off.'

Everybody left the ops room without uttering a single word. Vikas was standing in the ops room thinking about the possible task. 'It can't be Pakistan,' Vikas thought: 'then what? Is it China?'

'**H**urry up. Pack your stuff and put it in the vehicle,' Prashant commanded his company.

Prashant in his short service of two and half years had been given the task to command his company. Although he was the youngest company commander among all, the way he has managed his company in that exercise was admirable. He did not have much experience about the functioning of a company, but in these two and half years of service, he had always been part of one or the other competition. This helped him in knowing the men as well, as commanding and controlling them. It was not by authority of rank, but the logical reasoning of every class he had taken and drills which he had been taught and performed. Most of the troops were friendly with him at all times, except 0830hrs to 1230hrs when they were in training.

'Sahib are we going back today?' Raju asked.

'But we were supposed to have a picnic,' asked Saheb.

The third soldier was about to speak, but Prashant interrupted: 'yes we are going today, but not to our station.'

'Not to our station? Then where are we going?' Raju asked as he dismantled the tent pole.

'Even I don't know,' Prashant replied in a flat tone.

'Don't lie, Sahib, you are an officer. If you will give this type of reply, then how will we move ahead?'

'You are a leader Sahib, and our leader should know everything,' Saheb backed up Raju.

'Really I am not aware. I too only got to know this morning. Even I was preparing for the picnic,' Prashant said, defending himself.

'Prashant, don't chat around, tell them to pack and load as fast as possible,' Vikas said while taking a look around the whole area. He was getting things done as quickly as possible.

'Roger Sir,' Prashant said and turned towards the boys.

Before Prashant could say anything, all three said: 'just half an hour Sahib, and we will be finished.'

'Good,' Prashant tapped on Sahib's back, moved ahead and started shouting: 'hurry up, make it fast.'

It was only an hour after the orders were given and the whole fenced camp (half km) was taken down and packed. The CO came out of the tent and saw everything, called Vikas, whispered something and went back inside.

'Vikas for all officers, meet me at the entrance point, over,' Vikas transmitted the message on a radio set.

The camp was situated next to a road. The road leads to a picnic spot, and the hot spring, where many civilians used to go every day. The day Prashant's unit set up their camp, that area became the picnic spot. The selfies and photographs were at their peak, when a runner came with a written order from the CO to the civilians requesting: 'no photographs' and if taken 'not to be uploaded on any social media.' Though initially, the civilians could not believe It, as according to them, they were clicking with the real heroes of the nation. Later on, Uday intervened by saying: 'it's against the cyber law of the army, 'and then the civilians had to go back, disappointed. From that point on, for the next month, a message written on a blackboard ruined desires of many soldiers including Prashant's, who wanted to get themselves photographed with college girls, who used to come to the picnic area, until they saw the board saying: 'no photographs, defense area, vehicle parking prohibited.'

'Jai Hind Sir,' all three saluted Vikas.

'Right now, the CO has called me and asked me to get the things loaded as fast as possible. By tonight we have to reach Gangtok.'

'Gangtok?' Mohit asked in surprise.

'But sir, it's about 100km, and it will take 9 hours minimum,' Uday said.

'That's why; I am asking you to load the things in half an hour so that we can cover the distance in daylight. Right now, it's 0930hr, and I want the vehicles to be started by 1000hr. is that clear?'

'Roger Sir,' Mohit and Uday said.

'But sir, what about the lunch?' Prashant asked.

'Don't f*cking irritate me here. Tell them to pack, I don't care, and I want the vehicles to move by 1000hr. is it clear?' Vikas shouted loudly.

'Roger Sir, Jai Hind Sir,' Prashant said and disappeared.

The five soldiers working there slowly sped up the moment Vikas looked towards them. Now the whole camp had received some divine power. Everything was loaded into the vehicle. By 1010hr even the food was packed, and only a last quick check was required to if anything had been forgotten.

'Mohit, get everyone to fall in so that I can give the OK report to the CO,' Vikas said after walking the complete area.

'Roger Sir,' Mohit said.

Everybody was standing in the fall in ground and civilians' in their vehicles were moving and shouting 'Jai Hind' and saluting them.

'Sir, I guess India is really changing,' Prashant said standing next to Uday in fall-in.

'What do you mean?' Uday asked.

'See the effect of our PM Modi.'

'Don't joke around. The situation around me here is confusing, and your crazy talk is just an addition to it.'

'I mean; see people are paying respect and saluting us. It's the effect of Modi's "MAN KI BAAT" where he requested every citizen to salute whenever they see army personnel.'

'Have you ever traveled after commissioning?' Uday replied.

'What do you mean?' Prashant asked in confusion.

'Just say yes or no,' Uday said.

'In the last two years. I have traveled twice. Ah…and both times I flew. So, I haven't traveled by train.' Prashant said, recalling the details of his last two years leave.

'This time when you get leave, travel by train,' Uday said.

'Sir, why, and how is it related to MAN KI BAAT?' Prashant asked.

'This is directly related. Now listen.' Prashant started concentrating on Uday's statement.

Uday continued: 'see, by now you must have realized that it's not easy for any army personnel to plan his leave and go as per his plan.'

'That's true.'

'So, the moment you see that within a few days you are likely to get leave, you make a reservation.' Uday said.

'Definitely sir and I will try to get leave on Saturday,' Prashant said.

'So funny, when you make your reservation, you discover that you can't have a confirmed seat on the day that you had planned, because nowadays you need to reserve four months in advance. You have only one option left, and that is to travel without a reservation.' Uday explained.

'That's what most of us do because leave is important in life.'

'We all understand, and that's why we take that pain. Now with trains, it's straightforward to travel in the daytime even without a confirmed seat, but at night when you will approach TT for a seat reservation, he will charge you the highest price in the market. So, then you will use another ace move, that is, you will say that you are an army officer thinking that you have achieved something very high in life. He will simply say 'f*ck you' and sell the ticket to somebody else. Now you will have two options, either you go against your morals and use bribery, or you stand near a toilet. In my case, I choose to stand near the toilet.' Utter silence all around. It seemed there was a sequel of Bhagwat Gita going on where Uday was Krishna and Prashant was Arjun.

'Now, tell me where is the MAN KI BAAT EFFECT?' Uday continued: 'they are saluting you because they are comfortable in bolero, safari, and Innova (SUV cars) and you are rubbing your ass here. But the moment you move in their society and discomfort them a little, they will not give a f*ck about you. This is India, my brother. I am not saying that I have any problem, but this is a fact, and civilians are not ready to take any discomfort whatsoever for us.'

'But sir, we are very resourceful to them,' Prashant said.

'How?' Uday in confusion asked.

'Sir, frankly speaking whatsoever you have said is 100% right. Our civilian friends may not know where Kargil and Siachen are, but they know one thing.'

'What?' Uday asked.

'That; somebody is in the army, and he has an entrance to CSD canteen for cheap liquor,' Prashant commented

'That's true, and that is our mistake,' Vikas said.

'How?' Prashant asked.

'It is because we don't show them hardship. They only imagine us with CSD, toll-free and liquor cards; we get fooled very happily. Also, we make ourselves fools by offering them these resources just to hear them say "wow you are in the army, that's so great." They appreciate us a little, and we readily offer them our things.' Uday explained.

'That's true, one of my friends who has not talked to me since school days, have come to me and asked for some liquor and…?'

'And you gave it.'

'Yes, I gave it,' Prashant confirmed with a smile.

'I don't give my benefits to anyone. These are my hard-earned privileges, and I will never let any thankless person use them,' Uday said.

'Sir, then you might not have many friends I guess,' Prashant commented.

'I hate "friends with benefits" nobody visits my house or ask after my parent's health when I am not at my home, but the moment I go on leave many of them revolve around me. I really hate them.' Uday said in deep thought.

'**S**teady up,' Vikas commanded, and with that command, Prashant and Uday froze. Their discussion finished with this command.

'Jai Hind Sir,' Vikas saluted the CO, 'all ok Sir, the troops are ready to march.'

'At ease everyone,' the CO said. He paused for a second, and a drop of rain fell down on his cheek. The CO looked up, smiled and again looked towards the standing soldiers and said: 'I appreciate you all, for loading so quickly. Let me tell you all frankly, don't remain in any doubt whatsoever, we are not going to our peace station. I know you must be missing your wives, and kids but… the waiting period will increase now. At this time our nation needs us more than our loved ones, and this is what we all have signed up for. The exact location, even I have not been told, but tonight we have to reach Gangtok.'

The moment the CO said Gangtok, the rain started to pour down heavily. He paused and with a smile said: 'it's an auspicious day. Even god is bidding us farewell from this place. Without wasting even, a single second let's march. BHARATA MATA KI….'

'JAI,' the mountains rumbled, (Bharat Mata Ki Jai) and the sound echoed ten times. Everybody got into their vehicles.

'Prashant, you will be in the leading vehicle, Mohit the ninth, Uday in the eighteenth and I will be in the last vehicle. The CO's gypsy will move ahead of the convoy. Prashant, you will control the speed of the convoy. It should not move faster than 30km/hr. Stay in communication on the Motorola, on channel 5. Clear?' Vikas briefed the officers before climbing into the vehicle.

'Roger Sir,' all three shouted.

'Ok, then best of luck. Let's reach safety. Jai Hind.'

'Jai Hind Sir,' all three saluted and got into their allotted vehicle.

The convoy traveled for 1030hr. It was raining heavily. Mountains are beautiful for tourists, but for army personnel, a mountain is something else. It's a famous saying 'mountains eat troops.' And driving in the mountains is the biggest challenge for army vehicles. The army drivers, especially in the mountains: have to be ever alert. That because of not only for the safety of the troops they are carrying, but also to avoid any accidents with the civilian vehicles.

'Take out only your sleeping bags from the vehicle, have your dinner and then go to sleep,' Vikas ordered the troops, standing at the convoy ground in Gangtok.

The convoy had reached its destination on time. It was 1930hr when vehicles arrived, and everybody got to fall in, in half an hour. The journey was safe, with two short halts. Though the mountain sickness had troubled most of them causing headaches and vomiting; all replied 'ALL WELL' when asked about their health by the CO. It's a sort of drill that whenever the commanding officer or somebody else asks about their well-being, it's a single answer 'THIK HAI SAHAB' (everything is fine Sir).

'Sir, can I request something?' Prashant asked after everybody settled into their respective allotted beds. Actually, it was a transit camp where each room has three to four beds, and it was just for a matter of a few hours. So, none of them bothered about the conditions: the beds or the rooms.

'What do you want?' Vikas replied getting himself comfortable in shorts and slippers.

Prashant paused for a second, but then gathering some courage asked: 'Sir, it's Gangtok and right now the clock has just hit 2000hr, can we sneak out?'

'Please Sir, God has given us an opportunity. Who knows when will we get the chance next time to visit Gangtok?' Mohit seeing the opportunity added.

'Yes, that's a good idea,' Vikas said.

Everybody in the room was amazed. Uday had just entered the room when Prashant dared to ask the question and the way Vikas answered; put everyone in a state of shock.

'What happened?' Vikas asked, looking at everyone.

'Nothing Sir, actually we were not expecting that answer,' Prashant said.

'See guys, I am not a sadist. It's Gangtok. Let's go and have some Beer and Pork Momos,' Vikas said happily.

'Sir, what about the CO?' Uday asked.

'Do you want to take him along with us?' Vikas asked.

'No sir, but he will never agree,' Mohit said.

'So, who is going to inform him? We will take the vehicle, we will go, and we will return by 2230hr,' Vikas said.

'But what if he finds out? He has got so many sources,' said Prashant in a concerned tone.

'Don't worry about it, I will handle everything. It's Gangtok, and that amount of risk is worth taking. Now, we had better hurry up before I change my mind,' Vikas said.

'Uday, just inform the driver,' Vikas ordered.

'Roger Sir,' Uday said and went out.

Everybody took a quick shower, and within half an hour they left the camp.

'So, where are we going?' Vikas asked while entering his name and particulars at the main gate of the transit camp.

'Sir, I will check out on Google Maps,' Uday said.

'Sir, the M.G. road will be the best. It's just a twenty-minute drive, and we will get everything there,' Mohit said while sitting in the vehicle.

'Wow Sir, how do you know about this place? Have you been here before?' Prashant asked, closing the rear gate of the gypsy.

'I have heard from my civilian friends,' Mohit said.

'Sir, friends or girlfriends,' Prashant asked.

'Just shut up,' said Mohit in mock anger.

'Ok enough, Uday, search for it on Google Maps. Let's go,' Vikas said to the driver.

'Roger Sir,' Uday said. 'Pizza hut on M.G. road,' Uday typed into Google search and started navigating.

The M.G. road was bustling. There was a vast crowd, lighting, bars, and restaurants, everything one can imagine. The moment they saw the glimpse of M.G. road from the far end, they were mesmerized. The peace station was not much of lively place, and moreover, for the month, they had not seen so many varieties of faces, races, and surroundings. For a few minutes, they kept walking on M.G. road without even talking to each other. All of them were physically together, but mentally everybody was at different stores and bars at the same time.

'Where is the Pizza Hut?' Vikas asked, breaking the spell.

'Oh sorry, Sir, this way,' Uday said looking at the navigator.

'I hope you all have cash,' Vikas asked everyone. Everyone answered by blinking their eyes and nodding their heads.

Four of them entered the Pizza Hut, and Uday ordered several pizzas after checking out the menu. They sat down in a corner that was not too crowded.

'So, what else?' Vikas asked after settling on the chair.

'Sir, after this we will go to the pub and have the only beer: Densberg is very famous,' Prashant said.

Uday and Mohit brought their order to the table. Both of them pulled up a chair and sat down.

'Mohit, what do your civilian friends say about Densberg?' Asked Vikas taking a slice.

'Sir, I was about to say the same thing. After eating the pizza, each one of us must have at least one Densberg. It's very famous in Sikkim, and it's cheap too. I believe it costs somewhere near seventy rupees only,' Mohit said.

'Really, then I will definitely try one,' Vikas said.

'Sir, what do you think the reason we are here is?' Uday asked biting into his pizza.

'Even I don't know. I tried to search for the news. But they are not showing anything,' Uday said.

'But Sir, what is so critical that within a few hours we were told to mobilize, and even, the final destination hasn't been revealed?' Mohit asked.

'I don't know, if anything were so important, it would have been on the news. But I really don't know,' Vikas said finishing his pizza.

'Does anyone want to have more?' Uday asked.

Everybody shook their head. They paid and went to have beer and Momos.

'I think we should move, it's 2200hr now,' Vikas said.

'It was entertaining Sir, a good break, after so long,' Prashant said.

'Tomorrow 0500hrs the vehicles should leave. Mohit you have to drive,. I hope you are not drunk,' Vikas said looking towards Mohit, who was feeling dizzy.

'Roger Sir, it will be done, and I am not drunk. It will be a shame if I can't handle a small bottle of beer. It's just because I haven't drunk beer for a long time. I'm just a little dizzy.' Mohit defended himself.

'Ok, let's go. Tomorrow 0500hr.' Vikas said.

By 2230hr they were on their way back. Because of the long and tiring day and by the blessing of a bottle of beer everybody fell asleep quickly. Prashant fell asleep with his shoes on. Mohit set the alarm to 0430hr and also fell asleep.

'Yakusla, that's the place where we are going,' Vikas said lighting his cigarette.

After a few hours' sleep, the convoy set out early in the morning at 0500hrs. Though it was not raining clearly, there was no hope of a bright day either. The convoy halted after covering a distance of sixty kilometers. This distance could have been covered within an hour, but the convoy took four hours to cover it. The convoy was stopped, and a break for breakfast was given. Prashant, Mohit, and Uday gathered near Vikas's vehicle and started to eat their breakfast.

'But where is this Yakusla?' Uday asked taking a piece of Paratha from the Tiffin.

'It's in North Sikkim,' Vikas replied.

'I have only heard about Nathu La,' Mohit said.

'Nathu La is famous because of tourists. Had it not been a tourist place, you would not have heard about Nathu la either,' Vikas said exhaling the last puff of smoke.

'Yes, that's so true,' Mohit nodded.

'Prashant, what happened? Are you still hungover?' Uday asked.

'No Sir, I'm not. When we were coming, one of the civilians asked me in the traffic if we were going to war.'

'So, what did you reply,' Vikas asked.

'I asked him where was he coming from? So, he said that he has come with his college friends to visit Sikkim.'

'Yes, this place is heaven for tourists and especially if you are coming from Mumbai, Gujarat, etc.' Mohit intervened.

But Prashant didn't listen to Mohit and continued: 'I didn't want to answer him, but there was a beautiful girl whom I happened to see accidentally, in the same vehicle. I put my Ray-Bans on and gave a filmy dialogue.'

'What dialogue was it?' Uday asked washing his hands.

'We are doing what we get paid for. Actually, it was too hot where we were stationed, so we thought we should pay a visit to Sikkim, and that's why we are going. There is no war as such.'

'And did he believe you?' Vikas asked in surprise.

'And the girl?' Mohit added.

'He was very much convinced by whatever I have said and that girl...' Prashant took a pause, washed his hands and continued: 'that girl, I still can't forget her face, didn't even look at me. You know Vikas Sir.'

'What?'

'They all lie,' Prashant said.

'Who lied to you?' Uday asked.

'Everyone in the academy.'

'Why?' Vikas asked.

'The instructors used to say that when you wear stars, all the girls will fall for you. This statement used to be my motivation during training time,' Prashant said.

'Yes, that is a beautiful lie,' Vikas said.

'You are not so handsome that girls will fall for you,' Mohit commented.

'I know I am not handsome. Had I been handsome I would have been an actor, not in the army,' Prashant said, taking a long breath.

'Stop being so dismal, Prashant,' Uday said.

'I am not dismal. I am just cursing my stars. They don't give a damn either,' Prashant said.

'Don't worry Prashant; you will find a beautiful girl. I think we should move. We have to reach Yakusla. Let's go,' Vikas said.

A whistle was blown thrice, and all vehicles started off. Prashant started searching for Yakusla on the Google map. After trying for some time, he noticed that there was no signal. The moment they left Gangtok, the mobile signal followed them for a few kilometers, and then it gave up.

Prashant looking out from the passenger window, went into deep thought. 'What a beautiful place this is. Teesta stream, young Himalayan Mountain, and the beautiful greenery. Yaks can be seen all around, grazing, carefree. The tops of the hills are full of Buddhist mantras. This place is really a paradise for tourists. I wish I could buy some land or make a home in this isolated area. It's such a natural beauty.'

Prashant didn't realize when he fell into a deep sleep. The moment he woke up he felt embarrassed because he was a firm believer that passenger should not sleep. With an embarrassed smile; he asked the driver 'where are we?'

'Sahib, we are twenty kilometers short of Yakusla.'

He looked at the watch it was five pm. He had slept for more than five hours, and he couldn't believe it.

'What about lunch?' He asked the driver.

'Sahib, The CO Sahib ordered not to stop before Yakusla.'

'What is so urgent?' Prashant enquired.

'I have overheard that Chinese troops have entered our territory and have broken some bunkers. The unit present there have managed to stop them. But...'

'When did this happen?' Prashant interrupted.

'Three days ago, I guess. I am not sure, but they are making a road over there,' Driver said.

Prashant couldn't understand, he stopped listening to him the moment he saw two beautiful lakes through the light on the bend in the road. Prashant had seen this type of view in movies and photos, but a lake at 1300ft, with his own naked eyes was his first experience. Prashant did not give even an iota of thought to the Chinese; he was mesmerized by the beauty of Sikkim. It was June; most of the parts of India must be cursing the sun and the weather. And here was Prashant, in Sikkim who was wearing thermals and jackets, enjoying the young Himalayan Mountain with ice, streams, yaks, and lakes. It started to drizzle, and after some time there was heavy rain. There were many sharp turns for the next twenty kilometers the convoy took more time than usual to finally reach the Yakusla base.

'Jai Hind Sir, this is lieutenant Hemant. I have been sent to receive you and show you your location,' Hemant shouted to Vikas. Though he was carrying an umbrella and also wearing a rain hat, still he could not stop himself from getting wet.

'Jai Hind, this is Major Vikas. Is it far?' Vikas said stepping out of his vehicle. Vikas had already put on his rain hat. But the moment he stepped down, his shoes got soaked.

'Yes sir, it's a little far,' Hemant said.

'Can vehicle go there?' Vikas asked.

'Sir, the vehicle can go, but there are clear orders that no vehicle should go beyond this place.' Hemant informed them.

'That's all right. But we will not be able to pitch tents, how are we going to be accommodated?' Vikas asked.

'Sir, don't worry. I will recommend you to leave your luggage in the vehicle, and your men can occupy the tents which are already pitched.' Hemant replied.

'The tents are already pitched?' Vikas asked in confusion.

'Sir, actually the unit which was here has been sent for another task, and their tents have been left behind for your battalion,' Hemant explained.

'That's ok, I will transmit this on the radio,' Vikas confirmed.

'No problem Sir,' and Hemant started walking with his torch showing the direction to Vikas.

'Vikas, for all: no luggage to be taken down, only personal items and sleeping bag to be taken from the vehicles.' Vikas released the push button of radio and repeated the message.

All the station said: 'Roger that.'

Everybody was tired and wanted to sleep when they heard the message most of them insisted on staying in the vehicle itself because of the coziness. But after several 'swear words,' everyone, cursing silently, marched one behind the other and reached the location. It was cold and raining. Nobody bothered about dinner. Most of them just fell asleep. Only some managed to resist until they had removed their shoes and socks, their bodies relaxed, and everybody, putting their knees close to their chest and hands between their legs, fell asleep.

'CO for Vikas over,' the voice from the radio repeated.

'Sir, the CO wants to talk to you,' Hemant said pointing at the radio.

'Oh! Thanks. I was thinking of something,' Vikas said as he took the radio and said: 'Vikas for CO pass the message, over.'

'Officers, the conference will be tomorrow, 0800hr, all officers to be present.'

'Roger Sir,' Vikas said. The radio battery dried up with two beeps.

'The radio is also dead. Let's see how this place turns out?' Vikas walked to the camp location.

'I think I should leave, good night Sir.' Hemant sought permission.

'I should also catch some sleep. Good night, take care.'

Vikas passed a few instructions, got some reports, returned and went to sleep. Prashant, Mohit, and Uday also came with their sleeping bags. They all went to check on their companies and boys. After confirming that everybody was asleep, they returned and wished each other 'goodnight' and slept.

'Good morning Sir, I see we are not alone,' Prashant said to Vikas.

Prashant hadn't been able to sleep the whole night. It was not that he didn't want to, but his sleeping bag could hardly resist the cold outside.

'How was your night?' Vikas asked.

'Enchanting'

'What does that mean?'

'First time in my life I desired sunlight so badly. My sleeping bag could not help me so, I started chanting.' Prashant said.

'I guess gods favor you then.'

'Even I have started believing from this moment.'

'Wake them up and just go and talk to the boys. See if they are comfortable or not. The sun may hide anytime.' Vikas ordered.

'Sir, what about the conference?' Prashant asked.

'Look at your watch, it's still 0600hr, you have two hours or so. So; it's better you freshen up and wake these two sleeping beauties, then give me a report about the boys.' Vikas ordered.

'Roger Sir.'

Prashant went and woke up Uday and Mohit. Though he didn't receive a friendly welcome, the moment he uttered Vikas's order, everybody was ready to march.

'Jai Hind Sir,' Hemant said.

'I think I know you,' Prashant said.

'Oh! Yes, I saw you last night with Vikas Sir.'

'Sir this is lieutenant Hemant.'

'Hi, this is Captain Prashant.'

'How was your night Sir?' Hemant asked.

'Wow, it was wonderful, with wind and rain. It's a paradise in this month of summer,' Prashant said sarcastically.

'Things are just out of our reach,' Hemant said after a deep thought.

'Oh! So, are you from the holding unit?' Prashant enquired.

'Yes sir,' Hemant replied.

'That sounds interesting; can you please tell me what's going on?'

'Are you not aware?' Hemant asked with surprise.

'Nobody is aware. See our fate, we were planning picnics, and God has planned for other things. Leave it; just tell me what's happening here?' Prashant asked the question again with curiosity.

'Sir, can you see a hundred meters ahead of you,' Hemant said.

'I guess my eyesight is not so damaged. I can see men in uniform standing. In fact, I guess there are more than fifty,' Prashant said.

'Sir, you are right, there are more than fifty men standing face to face with Chinese troops.' Hemant said.

'And what about those tents? Do we have more than one unit?' Prashant asked.

'Sir, you are not the first unit,' Hemant replied.

'What?' Prashant was shocked.

'Sir, actually there are already three units placed, and you are the fourth one,' Hemant said.

'Now, I am really shocked. In this stretch of one kilometer, we have three other units as well. You want to say that there are 1600 to 1800 men over here.' Prashant asked.

'You are right sir,' Hemant said.

'Oh my god, what is the issue?' Now, Prashant was a little concerned.

'We have seen the sun after I guess more than a week.'

'You mean to say: it rains a lot over here. I really hate the rain.' Prashant said.

'Sir, you need to get organized. I hope you have brought enough jackets, clothes, shoes, and socks,' Hemant informed as per his prior experience.

'I have catered for only one month.'

'I would recommend, you to get enough jackets and clothes. Let's go to that place where the men are standing,' Hemant said.

'Ok, let's go.'

Prashant and Hemant had hardly taken a few steps, when Vikas messaged on the radio to all the officers: 'Vikas for all stations report to me, over.'

'Sir, what is that message all about?' Hemant asked.

'There is an officer's conference. That's why we were called,' Prashant replied.

'I have seen all the COs sitting at the Baba Mandir,' Hemant said.

'And what is that?' Prashant asked.

'There is a Baba Mandir at the top, not too far from this place. Besides that, there is an Ops room,' Hemant said.

'Well, that's fine. But what is Baba Mandir?' Prashant asked.

'Don't you know about Harbhajan Baba?' Hemant asked in surprise.

'No, I don't, why?' Prashant asked carelessly.

'But you should know about him,' Hemant replied, disappointed: 'even tourist come to Baba Mandir. It's very famous in Sikkim.'

'Oh, I am so sorry; can you please tell the story?' Prashant asked.

'Ok Sir, I will tell you. He got enrolled in 23rd Punjab battalion in February. 1966 as a sepoy. In 1966, the states of Sikkim and North Bengal were under the rage of great natural catastrophe where landslides, floods, and heavy rain had taken thousands of lives across the two states. On October 4, 1968 sepoy Harbhajan Singh was escorting a mule caravan from his battalion headquarters in Tukula to Dengchukla. He fell into a vast flowing stream and drowned. It was on the fifth day that he was missing that his colleague Pritam Singh had a dream of Harbhajan Singh informing him of this tragic incident and his dead body being buried under a heap of snow, Harbhajan Singh also desired to have a Samadhi made after him. Pritam Singh ignored the dream as just imagination, but later when the body of sepoy Harbhajan Singh was found at the same spot where Harbhajan Singh had informed, the army officials were taken aback. As a mark of respect towards his wish, a Samadhi was constructed near Chhokyachho. Baba Harbhajan Singh warns of dangerous activities on the border through the dreams of army men, even Chinese army personnel claim to have seen a human figure patrolling in the night across the border. Baba Harbhajan Singh is now honored with the rank of Honorary Captain.'

'Wow, I was really not aware of the story,' Prashant said.

'And you know what Sir?' Hemant asked.

'What?' Prashant said.

'In his honor, no army personnel are supposed to have meat or liquor on Sunday,' Hemant told him.

'That means; Sunday is considered as Baba's day in the army,' Now, Prashant understood the story.

'You are right Sir,' Hemant said.

'Hemant, it was nice talking to you. I wish to hear more stories, but I have to go. If you wish you can join us for breakfast,' Prashant said.

'Sir, thanks for offering. Sorry to refuse Sir, but I have already had my breakfast.'

'Ok, see you then.'

'Jai Hind Sir,' Hemant saluted.

'Jai Hind, take care,' Prashant also saluted and started walking towards his tent.

'What took you so long? We could not resist so, we have eaten; now take your plate and have some breakfast,' Mohit said, he was holding his plate with Poori and Sabzi on it.

'Wow, breakfast: Poori and Sabzi,' Prashant picked up his plate and started eating.

'Where have you been?' Uday asked.

'Sorry for keeping you waiting, but I was chatting with lieutenant Hemant, the officer who came to receive us last night,' Prashant said.

'But I didn't see any officer last night,' Mohit said.

'Same here,' Uday said.

'He is right, last night he came to receive us. I met him, and then he was with me, that's why maybe you guys have not seen him.' Vikas cut in, 'how are the boys? This is more important than who met Hemant and who didn't

All three understood the mood of Vikas. 'Sir, things are not fine,' Uday said.

'That's what I am asking, what are the problems?' Vikas asked.

'Sir, we could somehow manage breakfast, but we have to set up camp,' Mohit said.

'Have you told someone?'

'Yes Sir, I have told Subedar Babu. Under his observation camp will be set up in one hour or so.'

'Sir, apart from the camp there is another problem.'

'What is it?'

'Sir, we don't have any water. The boys have taken out water by pressing the grass, plants, and soil for morning obligations,' Mohit explained the problem.

'This is not good. But why is there no water have you enquired?' Vikas asked, taking a long drag of his cigarette.

'Sir, I have enquired about it, the officer who is responsible said that he needs to locate a different water source. He was not ready for such a large quantity of men. He had catered only for one battalion, and now he is facing the problem because there are four battalions.'

'I will have to discuss this with the CO. but what about now?'

'Sir, our boys are fetching water in buckets from neighboring battalions.' Mohit said.

'Let us wait for the CO. It's already half past eight. He should have come by now. I don't know where he is. I tried to contact him on the radio.'

'The CO is in a conference since this morning,' Prashant said putting his plate down.

'How do you know?' Mohit asked.

'Hemant told me.'

'Did he tell you anything about the situation?' Vikas asked throwing the cigarette butt away.

'Not much. But he said; there are four battalions over here, and he has shown the disputed area.' Prashant said.

'What disputed area?' Uday asked.

'Four battalions at this place, oh my god, I cannot believe this,' Mohit was amazed.

'You guys have made this tent a smoking chamber. I can hardly breathe,' the CO, commented as he entered the tent.

'Jai Hind Sir,' all stood up and saluted together.

'Jai Hind gentlemen, sit down wherever you find a place,' the CO sat on one of the beds, everybody got settled down. Prashant stayed standing.

'I am coming directly from the conference. I will tell you what is happening here. Prashant, can you please just ask for tea,' the CO ordered.

'Roger Sir,' Prashant said and went outside. He sent a runner for tea and returned to the tent. The CO started talking when Prashant had returned.

The CO continued: 'this is a serious problem what we have right now. This is Yakusla plateau, where we are right now. The Chinese are trying to make a road through this area. They have destroyed two bunkers and have brought dousers. The holding unit's men stood in the way and also brought a douser in one night and placed it just opposite to their douser. This happened 10 days ago, and now we are at the faceoff,' the CO explained the whole situation.

'Sir, but nothing is being shown on the news,' Vikas said.

'News channels have been stopped at Gangtok as they are not allowed to move up. I guess the media does not know much about this,' the CO said.

'But Sir, it has already been 10 days, how long will it take?' Mohit asked.

'See, there was face-off earlier also, but it didn't last long. I guess in the next ten to fifteen days it will be over. There will be one or two flag meetings, and it will be over.' The CO said hopefully.

'Sir, but there are so many battalions,' Prashant said.

'It's one of our policies to show a larger strength. It has worked many times, and we are following the same strategy here, that's why' the CO said.

'But Sir, how does the road affect us?'

'If this road goes to Bhutan, as China wants, then they will be able to dominate the Siliguri corridor, and the whole northeast may get cut off.' The CO expressed his concern.

There was a silence in the tent after that statement.

'How are the boys? Are they comfortable?' the CO broke the ice.

'Sir, they are fetching up stores, right now there is only one problem, that is the water,' Vikas said.

'So, do we have a solution?'

'Sir, Uday has talked with the officer-in-charge, and he has assured him that by evening he will resolve this issue.'

'Ok then, I will take your leave. I will have to go to a conference in the evening again. Get yourselves comfortable, get TV and keep track of the news, and if that water issue does not get solved by evening, let me know. Bye,' the CO said as he walked out of the tent.

'Jai Hind Sir,' Vikas went outside to see.

'Sir, I could not understand anything.' Prashant said.

'Why are you worrying Prashant?' Vikas asked.

'But Sir, is this War or Peace? Really, I can't understand,' Mohit said.

'Just calm down, watch some TV and visit the boys once.' Vikas avoided the question. He took out his phone and started playing the football game.

'**G**ood morning sir,' Prashant said as he entered the tent.

'Good morning Prashant. Come and help me out,' Vikas said with a smile.

'How can I help you?'

Prashant sat down near Vikas who was busy with pen and paper.

'I am actually calculating the manpower as per duties and requirements,' Vikas said.

'I can help Sir, but I am afraid I am not aware of the duties over here,' Prashant said.

'You will come to know later but right now just understand where we have to put sixty men standing at a time alongside the fences.' Vikas explained.

'Sir, but I guess we have 200 men more or less.'

'That is the problem. If we exclude the camp staff and a few for some contingencies then we have to make three groups,' Vikas said.

'Sir, but it's difficult. If we make three groups that means; 8 hours duty per day, per group.' Prashant thought twice and said.

'Yes, and the problem is if any one of them gets ill or something else, what then?'

'Then we have to take out the boys from camp.'

'You know Prashant, it is easy to calculate on paper, two hundred divided by sixty, three groups and eight hours per day but on the ground, it is difficult and a little harsh also.' Vikas said.

'I could not get it, sir,' Prashant said.

'Anybody will say it is an easy job. But if you think like a human, a person standing for eight hours and then he has to do other work, as well as his own daily routine....'

'Yes sir, you know my uncle says that Faujis cannot do anything good apart from standing. I ignored him when he said that. Nobody can understand the pain of a soldier in this nation.'

'Sir, since the weather is clear the CO is calling everyone,' Mohit said as he entered the tent.

'But why?' Vikas asked.

'Sir, for area familiarization,' Mohit said.

'Ok, let us go and familiarize ourselves.' Vikas had put down his pen and paper and moved out.

It has been two days since the day they had reached Yakusla, and it had been raining continuously. Except for the sleeping bag, there was no relief for them. Wind and rain were a deadly combination. That morning was a very bright morning, and the whole Yakusla plateau was visible.

'Jai Hind Sir,' Vikas said.

'Come gentlemen, good morning to you all. Let me familiarize you with the terrain.'

Everybody started looking towards the direction where the CO was pointing his finger.

'Gentlemen, we are standing right now at lower Yakusla. You can see, to our east, we have Bhutan, in North China. Actually, according to the international boundary, China is quite far from this place, but China claims this land as their part, and we support Bhutan as this is Bhutan's territory. Look north you can see the Indian flag, and from there along with the same ridgeline turn east, the topmost feature is called Guruji. From Guruji, up to our position and towards the south you can see the topmost feature that is called Dada. From Guruji to Dada is the alignment of the international boundary. This is based on the concept of a watershed. Since this is Bhutan's territory, you can see we have just fenced in with barbed wire, unlike the Pakistan border. You can see two lakes on the left of Dada; those lakes are in Bhutan territory. Does anybody have any doubt?' the CO asked.

'Sir, I can see some dozers far on the skyline in the northeast,' Prashant said.

Everybody looked towards the direction in which Prashant pointed.

'Oh! Excellent observation, you can see it's a sort of wall at the far end. That is the place from where they are making a road, and then they intend to come down and make the road to 'Dada' and then further into Bhutan.'

'Have they already constructed a road behind that?' Vikas asked.

'Yes, our intelligence report says that they have already made a class 40 road to that place and now they are moving ahead.'

'But sir this is Bhutan's territory. What interest do we have?' Uday asked.

'Can you see some soldiers standing over there?'

'Yes sir, both nations men are standing face to face.' Mohit said.

'That is the face-off point. They have stopped the Chinese troops from moving ahead of that point, and if they move ahead and make the road, then our Siliguri corridor and whole north-east will be in danger.'

'But sir, China claims the road as a part of their economic plans. One road one trade type,' Prashant said.

'That is one of the main mottos. For them, it may be traded, but for us, it is a danger towards our sovereignty. Actually, India and China had signed a treaty in 2012 to maintain the status quo.'

'Sir, what is status quo.?' Prashant asked in confusion.

'It says that no changes in geography will be done over here by either side. But they are changing by making a road, and we are forced to take action.'

'Sorry to disturb you, Sir, I have worked out duties and manpower,' Vikas interrupted.

'Let us go inside and talk.'

Vikas and the CO went back to the tent. Prashant, Uday, and Mohit started looking at the beautiful plateau.

'Sir, see there are so many small lakes all around.' Prashant said.

'Yes, it is a magnificent place.' Uday said.

'Sir, we are standing at more than 12000ft nearly 14000ft. But we can see the tree line. I thought that the tree line would disappear after 9000ft, that is what I have read.' Mohit said.

'That is true. After 9000ft the tree line starts disappearing, but that is in J and K (Jammu & Kashmir) and Ladakh region. This is beautiful Sikkim, and that is why you are not having any problem with breathing. Otherwise, at 12000ft and above, most of the places have less oxygen.'

'Sir, look over there, the Chinese are rotating their duty. I think they are carrying QBZ-95.' Prashant said.

'Yes, that is correct. That is their assault rifle,' Uday said.

'Are they carrying ammunition?' Mohit asked.

'That I am not aware of. I don't see a magazine on their weapons. But one thing I know that after 1967, I don't think either nation have fired any bullets towards each other. There are no firing orders from both the sides and both the nations are following to date.'

'Sir, was it 1962 or 67?' Prashant asked.

'1962 Sino-Indian (China and India) war, everybody is aware of, but in 1967 there was conflict in Nathu La, and the Chinese lost it.'

'Oh! I thought 1962 was the first and only.'

'Ninety-five percent people think the same, but they are not aware of 1967.'

'Sir, you know what is the problem in India?' Mohit said.

'What?' Uday asked.

'We do not document our things. See America or other nations, they glorify their army. I guess everybody knows about their armies and wars and so on. But in our country, we will not move ahead of love stories. I think somebody should make documentaries on our wars and conflicts.'

'But that will not be sold sir,' Prashant interrupted.

'I am not talking about making a profit.'

'No profit, no work. This is India, my brother. You should be thankful that you are being paid even after doing purely non-economical work,' Uday said.

'Sir, but...' Mohit defended.

'You should not forget that you are standing against the country whose army is not only larger, but their defense budget is ten times greater than ours.'

'You know Sir, what we are best at?' Prashant asked.

Mohit and Uday looked clueless.

'Debates and proof of everything, don't you remember the surgical attack where our own leaders asked for proofs? Let us leave the topic and go and have breakfast. I am feeling starving.' Prashant said.

'Me too,' Mohit said.

'Yes, that is right. Napoleon has said "an army marches on its stomach," so, we need to eat. Let us go,' Uday said. All three went towards their tent. The flag was waving; men were standing, and at the far end dozers and cranes were doing what they were supposed to do.

'**S**ir, what are you cooking?' Prashant asked.

It had been more than a week since they had arrived at Yakusla. Initially, there was the problem of water and other things, but in a day or two, those things had been catered for. Even the rain could not stop the will of a soldier to make themselves comfortable. The beauty of the army is that they can settle down in any terrain. Just a few days are required to adapt. The difficulty of working and complaints are sorted at 1030 tea, 1230 lunch, 1600 tea, and 1830 dinner. If these few demands are taken care of nothing is impossible for the army.

'Hi Prashant, come and sit.' Vikas said as he stirred the pot.

'Sir, but what are you cooking in this 6 by 4-foot bunker?' Prashant was curious to know.

The bunker was made up of hollow blocks, and few pieces of the hollow block were lying around. Vikas was sitting on a hollow block, and he was focusing on the pan which was placed on the stove. Prashant looked around, took one of the hollow blocks and sat near Vikas.

'Can you please pass me that oil, just behind you?' Vikas said.

'This room is so cozy. It is freezing out there, and I do not think rain is going to stop.'

'Hmm,' Vikas just nodded without showing any concern. 'Pass me chicken, now I think it is a right time and all spices are mixed properly.'

Prashant gave him the chicken which had already been washed and was being kept in a small bucket.

'When did you learn to cook, Sir?' Prashant asked.

'Being married teaches you a thousand things, and this is the first of all.'

'Oh! So, madam taught you.'

'No, it is not her; it is my 'Majboori' (helplessness) which has taught me. Do you know how to cook?' Vikas asked.

'No Sir, I don't even know how to make tea.'

'Then I am advising you. It is better to learn now; otherwise, life is not easy my friend.'

Prashant did not say anything. Vikas's concentration over the cooking got disturbed because of Prashant's silence. Vikas looked towards Prashant who seemed terrified and said 'don't worry, marriage is not so horrifying. I was just joking. You know every man should learn to cook. It is not just women's thing.'

'Yes, that I agree. But it is complicated for me. I tried at home, but could not learn it.'

'There is nothing to learn. It is not rocket science. It is just practice and experience.'

'But Sir, when did you learn?'

'Frankly speaking, it was after marriage, but not because of my wife. Actually, I started accompanying her in the chopping of vegetables and watching the cooker's timer. One fine day I tried to surprise her by cooking myself but that thing turned into a disaster, but then, she appreciated my effort. It was just appreciation, nothing more than that, she didn't even touch the food. I had to clean the mess up and then had to order from outside. But after that, I learned.'

'So, can you cook all types of meat dishes?'

'No, I still cannot cook fish, it is difficult. But she likes mutton curry which I can now cook.'

'Wow, Sir that is so nice. I guess I need to learn to cook as early as possible.'

'Yes, you should. You know it is the best pass time. Whenever your mood is upset, get yourself in the kitchen and try to cook something. You will enjoy it.'

'Definitely, I will try.'

'This cooking thing helped me when she was pregnant. I could give her homemade food.'

Prashant nodded.

'Taste this soup,' Vikas took out a spoon of soup and gave it to Prashant to taste.

'Sir, it is perfect. Really you cook far better than our trained cooks.'

'Thanks, buddy. It is actually your madam's recipe. She taught me. I don't know whether chicken pieces are well cooked or not.' Vikas pressed a few pieces with the spoon with expertise and said again 'you know it is difficult to cook over stove and pan. It is straightforward in a cooker, one just requires a timer, and that is it.'

'I don't know much Sir,' Prashant said in embarrassment: 'Sir, Nisha must have turned one?'

'Yes, she is now one year and two months. You know when she first said 'papa' your madam got very annoyed. Every day I wonder if when I go home whether she will be able to recognize me or not. It has been more than one month now, and I just pray she comes to my lap the same way she used to come a month back. You know, whenever I used to park my car, she used to crawl out of the room for me.'

Prashant looked at Vikas's face. A tear rolled down from Vikas's eye, and which even Vikas did not try to wipe away. Every day he was controlling his tears, and that drop seemed to be a burden for his eyes to hold. Even the army personnel have the right to get emotional, to cry.

For Prashant, it was the first time he had seen any army officer so emotional, in fact, since his training academy to date, he thought army officers did not have any emotions. Even he had heard that Vikas was a very emotionally and physically active officer, but his daughter had melted him so much that it became challenging to maintain his persona. Vikas tried to avoid eye contact with Prashant. Prashant sensed Vikas's unease, and to change the topic said 'Sir I think the chicken is ready to be served.'

Vikas took a deep breath and said 'Oh! Yes, I think it is ready now. Let us go, just tell Gautam to get chapattis and rice from camp. In half an hour we will have dinner.'

'That is fine Sir. I will tell Gautam. Let us go and watch TV, and see if anything or any news about this place is hitting the headlines or not.'

'**S**ir, Cigarette.' Uday offered a cigarette to Vikas.

'Light it up, we will share. Is there any news about Yakusla?' Vikas asked, sitting on the only chair kept in the tent.

All four officers were sharing the tent, and after the T.V. had been installed, there was space left only for one chair in that tent. The tent was full not because of beds and luggage but because of the mini office which they agreed to open in the same tent. Though it had eased their job, they had to compromise with space. They did not seem to be so worried about space because every time one or the other officer had to stand with the boys at stand-off. They used to gather all together, just for dinner.

'Even we were eagerly searching for it Sir,' Mohit said.

'Sir, it has been more than 15 days, and India is not aware of this,' Prashant who was standing in a corner complained.

'Maybe it is a policy to deal with the situation. Most of the time the media blackout solves many issues,' Vikas said, switching the channels.

'And especially a country like India, which has such liberal media, should remain out of this. Otherwise, they will start a debate,' Uday added.

'How are the boys?' Vikas asked.

'They are confused. They don't understand why they are here?' Prashant said.

'They are anxious about how long will it take?' Uday said.

'So, what did you answer?' Vikas asked.

'Sir, we explained the reason why we are here, and we have also told them it will be over shortly,' Mohit said.

'If the media is not showing anything that means either Delhi is not aware of the matter, or that it has been resolved, and we will shortly receive orders of de-inducting,' Prashant said.

'Sir, I don't think we have a strong foreign policy,' Uday said, crossly.

Vikas sensed Uday's disappointment. To calm him Vikas said: 'let us play a game.'

'What game Sir?' Everybody asked.

'The game's name is what if?'

Everybody seemed confused.

'Don't get confused. You all are the P.M. right now, and you will give me a solution one by one, to this problem.'

'Sir, please we need some elaboration,' Prashant requested.

'You know that the Chinese have come up and we are standing face to face to stop them from gaining further progress. It has been more than 15 days, and the P.M. has not taken any steps. What would you do if you were the P.M.?'

The three of them looked at each other.

'Ok, Mohit what would you do?' Vikas initiated seeing the confusion.

'Sir, I would continue in the same way,' Mohit answered.

'That means stand-off.'

Mohit nodded his head in affirmation.

'Uday you?'

'the same Sir, I would wait for some diplomatic posture.'

'Ok, and you Prashant?'

'Sir, I would wage war,' Prashant answered, 'so you will wage war, that is interesting. Now, can you explain to me your plan?'

'Sir, I know that enemy is at our gates, and after a few talks, they are not going back. So, seeing this as a failure I will open diplomatic channels and be taking Bhutan into my confidence I will order them to fire and then I will go to the U.N. and ask for justice because my act would be in defense of my sovereignty.'

'Good. Now you see this issue has been going on for more than 15 days and even Bhutan has not given any statement. Suppose that Bhutan denies supporting you. It may say that they are there and they don't want a third party like India to get into the issue.'

'But all supplies in Bhutan are dependent on India. I would cut off everything.'

'Then that will be a win-win situation for China. You cut off your supply and China will start feeding them. That is what they did with Nepal. Nepal and China are closer friends than India-Nepal, though we share many common interests. Do you agree?'

'Yes, Sir.'

'Then, what else?'

'Still, I will go to the U.N. and since we have ties with America and our ties are increasing with Russia, we have a historic relationship they can help, and this will isolate China politically.'

'Russia will not help because China and Russia share the same thoughts of communism. Yes, they may not go against India, but openly they will not support us either. Now, your next new friend: America. Are you aware that a lot of Chinese money is involved in America's Stock market in the form of shares?'

'No sir.'

'The moment America supports you, China will withdraw all of its stock, and the American economy will collapse within a minute. It is not Pakistan which is dependent on America. So, I don't think America is going to take that risk just for new friends and India is not even part of NATO either. What else?'

Prashant tried to speak but was speechless. Even Uday and Mohit had nothing to say.

'Ok, leave America on this topic. The day that you wage war, The Chinese will first attack your stock markets and satellites, then all your systems will be hacked. Your whole system will collapse. Your opponents will come on the road protesting against you, and your government will be thrown out. For all this, you will be held responsible. The country's economy which has just taken pace will again collapse, and your whole political carrier will be burnt by your own people. Now tell me will you risk so much?'

'I don't know Sir,' Prashant said, quietly.

'So, whatsoever is going on let it be in the same way because that is the right way for now and you know why we played this game?'

'No Sir,' Uday said.

'Because, you all seem disappointed with the higher-ups and their decisions, and if you are disheartened and disappointed, the boys will never be able to do their work, because the boys don't know the P.M., politics, and everything. They just know that you are their company commanders and if you are happy here, then they are as well.'

All three could not utter a word. They looked down towards their toes and started thinking.

'Oh! Come on. Let us not make the chicken wait,' Vikas spoke in a cheerful tone 'I want this chicken to be finished. Come Prashant, take charge of serving the chicken.'

'Sahib, do you know? In many ways: The Chinese are better,' Sub Babu said.

Prashant and sub-Babu were standing near a bunker. The road behind that had come up approximately 200 meters ahead of the wall and dozers were continuously doing the job. Now, it has become a hobby for them to stand and observe Chinese dozers working.

'How can you say that?' Prashant asked.

'It has been a month, and the Chinese have not fired even a single bullet.'

'But that is because of our treaty with China.'

'For a country like, China, how much time does it take to break the treaty?'

'That is also true.'

'I imagine it was not Pakistan.'

'I have not seen Pakistan. But Babu Sahib you must have served more than 15 years in front of China, out of your 28 years of service.'

'On account of my experience, I am telling you this.'

'Can you tell me more?'

'You were talking about the treaty and trust; I will share with you one incident.'

Prashant started listening carefully. Sub Babu continued: 'Sahib you know Pakistan always has a ruthless policy. In northern Kashmir, we have the same situation somewhat like this. Pakis and our bunker face each other just the same eyeball to eyeball. It snows a lot in Kashmir and its northern region, because of which the bunkers get covered. Our troops have to maintain the area for communication and patrolling. Just 50 meters ahead of us there is Paki's bunker. There was a mutual understanding between the troops and commanders of both sides. Both sides used to put the white flags in the morning and come out for the snow clearance, and by afternoon the flag used to be taken down, and everybody used to go to their bunkers. This was just a local, peaceful, agreement that we used to follow. One fine day the same drill started. Our soldiers keeping their weapons and ammunition in the bunker came out for snow clearance. Pakis also came out, looked at them and then suddenly rushed back to their bunker and opened fire. Before our troops could react, all four of them died.'

Prashant was utterly shocked, and he asked 'then?'

'Our post was cut off. But the moment the battalion got to know about this incident, the battalion commanders launched an operation and captured that Pakistani post. Pakis by that time had already left the post. Though the bunker was captured, the battalion had lost 4 men, it is not worth dying. The Pakis breached our trust and faith, and we try to maintain Aman ki Asha (Hope of peace).'

'That is really inhuman.'

'Humanity is not there in Pakis. They are never taught humanity in life. They are only preached that every Indian is their enemy and they should kill them.'

'But do you know Sahib?'

'What is that Sahib?' Sub Babu asked

'The existence of Pakistan is only on the hatred of India.'

'I don't get it, Sahib.'

'I will explain it to you. Like for China, India is one of the many problems. It has to look after 15 countries around it but for Pakistan raising Kashmir issue is the only way to let the World know of their existence.'

'Yes, that is right. But Sahib, whenever we get posted to the Pakistan border, we must remain cautious.'

'Babu Sahib, thanks for this wonderful lesson. You know Sahib, reading and gaining a degree is a different thing, but it can never beat experience. And, you know what; young officers like me should always be guided by people like you. That is how we learn and lead.' Prashant shook his hand firmly and even hugged sub-Babu out of respect.

Prashant heard from somewhere: 'Hey captain Kabir, Kabir.'

Prashant looked at the place from where he was being called. Prashant waved his hand and started moving towards captain Wang.

'Ni Hao,' Prashant greeted.

'Good, hi' Wang replied.

'Your troops were saying that they don't know any captain Kabir,' Wang enquired.

'Oh! Yes. I mean, I have come from the young officer's course. So, not many of them know me well,' Prashant replied with a smile, trying not to reveal his secret.

'Young officer course, what is that?'

Prashant sensed that he could convince him, said: 'actually when we pass out and go to our battalions. After a few months, we are sent to the young officer course where they teach us platoon and company tactics, and after that, we go for the commando course. So overall it takes approximately eight to nine months. That is why many of the boys don't know me by my name, but they know me by face.'

'But in my opinion, it is not good for a leader that his subordinates don't know his name,' Wang said.

Prashant was finally assured that Wang was convinced about his fake identity. Making a sorry face, he said: 'sorry Sir, this will not happen again, and I will ensure that they at least know my name.'

'Apology accepted.'

They both burst into laughter.

'What happened that day? Why your boss was serious, and he got these sandbags filled,' Prashant pointing towards the said sandbags which were placed on the very first day they met.

'Oh! These sandbags! These are in response to the trenches which have been dug.' Wang said.

'But we did not dig any trenches.' Prashant said.

'My boss showed the photographs that Indians are digging trenches, so we had to respond. We felt threatened.' Wang said.

'Can you look back towards your area? You are digging trenches.'

'Where?'

'Just look back, within 15 days you have made 3 bunkers and a proper communication trench, and then you say that you are feeling threatened,' Prashant's tone changed. He spoke as if he was standing in some colony of India where neighbors fight over small issues with each other.

'I am really not aware. I was not here. I had gone to Nathu La for a flag meeting, and I came today. The first thing I did was come to look for you. I guess we are not friends anymore,' Wang was disappointed.

Prashant felt very sorry for himself. In the last statement, he forgot how happy he had felt when Wang called for him. He felt very disappointed and said: 'I am a very sorry friend. I guess it's the stress because of the situation.'

'Friends don't say sorry. I can understand,' Wang put his hand on his shoulder and said: 'leave it. I have brought a few chocolates for you.'

'Wow, Chinese chocolates. Thank you very much.'

Prashant and Wang opened the chocolate wrapper and put it in their mouth. 'It is very delicious. Thank you once again,' Prashant said.

Wang gave the chocolate to the boys standing there on duty. They looked towards Prashant. Prashant blinked his eyes as a gesture of 'yes.'

While enjoying the chocolate, Prashant crushed the wrapper, but suddenly he opened it; as he noticed something written on the wrapper: that he wanted to read.

Except the "Made in China," everything was written in Chinese on the chocolate wrapper.

'Ha, ha, ha... made in China,' Prashant looked at the wrapper and commented.

'Yes, it's a Chinese product and a famous brand,' Wang replied.

'Hey, why you people are everywhere? Why is "Made in China" almost everywhere in the World? I mean in India more than 90% electronic products say: made in China.' Prashant eagerly asked in a breath.

'Hmm, it's all about Mass Production, Dumping, and Highly Productive Labor,' Wang answered with pride and confidence.

'What?' Prashant shouted a little in a shock as he couldn't understand.

It was jargon for Prashant; he never heard something like this.

'Mass production... Dumping... What is that?' Prashant asked curiously.

Wang explained: 'Mass production is about the massive or huge production and manufacturing; mass production in a huge quantity or in bulk.'

'Dumping is a term used in international trade when a country or company exports a product at a price that is lower in the foreign importing market than the price in the exporter's domestic market. It occurs when manufacturers export a product to another country at a price below the normal price. It is also called Pricing Policy. When a

Chinese company goes to another country, it ruins the local market there. This is called dumping.' Wang explained.

Prashant's eyes and mouth were left open; he could not say anything for a few seconds.

'Wow, good to know. That's why China is one of the strongest economies.' Prashant said, after thinking.

'Yes, of course, even China is the most populated nation in the World,' Wang said.

'I think it is only because of the cheap labor cost in China,' Prashant commented.

'Excuse me, who told you that? Chinese labor is not cheap; it is cost effective and highly productive. Our government has actually enabled skill development in the country.' Wang replied in a loud voice.

'Our government helps and promotes the leading corporations to capture the international market. The Chinese government also helps in business expansion for future growth, development, and export.' Wang explained.

'Ok, that's the reason; in India, our media is against the Chinese products, and people have started avoiding the Chinese products.' Prashant said.

'No, your media can't do anything. China is the global hub of manufacturing; more than 60% of the most luxurious international brands are manufactured in China. Today, China is the global factory of the World.' Wang commented.

Prashant did not have a word to say; as he knew that the dirty politics in India were just for winning the elections. The political parties, the leaders, the opposition and the media fight together that is how they would get votes in the next elections after five years?

There was a silence for a minute; Prashant was thinking about the enormous differences between India and China, while China is a neighboring country.

'What happened?' Wang broke the silence.

'Hmm, skill building is also initiated in India by the government, I hope it will work,' Prashant said.

'What about your leave?' Prashant asked.

'Leave. What leave?' Wang asked.

'There must be some policy of leave like in one year after so many days you can take leave.' Prashant explained.

'Oh! Yes. It is there. It is like if we are at the peace station, then we get 30 days of compulsory leave in one year and if we are placed in the places like these, then 90 days,' Wang said.

'Wow, when did you go on leave last time?'

'This year, I have not been able to take leave.'

'Why?'

'These leaves are only on paper. It is hard to get actual leave.'

'I think that is the problem worldwide.'

'Why? Have you also not had any leave?'

'Sadly, zero days, we also have the same policy.'

'All soldiers share the same problem everywhere,' Wang said in a sad tone.

'That is why I am saying: You also go back and I also go back. Let's leave this place.'

'No, you go first.'

'No, you go first.'

They both repeated more than 10 times the same sentence. They seemed like they were the school students who are fighting over a pencil or eraser. The way they were talking, it didn't appear as if they were a part of such an essential problem between the two countries.

'What happened in the flag meeting?' Prashant asked

'Nothing positive for both of us, both the parties said they would talk to higher-ups. I don't know what will happen, winter is coming.' Wang feeling the cold wind said.

'Do you watch Game of Thrones?'

'What is that?' Wang asked.

'Don't you know Game of Thrones? It is a T.V. series. It is a very famous English series,' Prashant said.

'I don't know. But why did you ask that?' Wang asked.

'Because you said 'winter is coming' and it is the famous dialogue of this series,' Prashant replied.

'Oh! Do you have this series?'

'I have it on my downloaded on my hard drive.'

'Can you give it to me?' Wang asked.

'Sure, I will get my hard drive,' Prashant said with a smile of assurance.

'No not right now,' Wang said.

'Why?' Prashant asked.

'Because this is my dinner time and after that, I have a duty at night,' Wang said.

'But it is only five p.m. why would you have dinner so early?' Prashant looking at his wristwatch said.

'That is in India, not in China,' Wang replied.

'Oh, sorry I forgot. Bye, see you tomorrow.'

Prashant and Wang walked in opposite directions, but Prashant moved with a smile on his face. He was really enjoying the company of his enemy.

'Babu Sahib; who are those people?' Prashant pointed his finger towards the far distance where on the ridgeline silhouettes of many could be seen.

'Sahib, those are the people who are calling,' Sub Babu replied.

'Calling, but how? Is there any network?' Prashant asked.

'At particular places, mobile receives BSNL network and through that people are communicating,' Sub Babu said.

'Have you ever been there? It is because I was not aware' Prashant asked.

'I tried my luck once.'

'What do you mean luck?'

'Sahib, actually I tried to search the network for half an hour and then after that when my number got registered, I tried to call which again took five more minutes because the network was too busy and after trying fifty times, it rang once, and nobody picked up. So, it was hard luck for me, and after that, until now I have not gone. Our boys go and talk there,' Sub Babu explained.

'But when do they go there?' Prashant asked.

'Whenever they go for rations and other things,' Sub Babu replied.

'Oh! That's why there is such a crowd. It has been almost a month, and now I recall that I have not called my home. I will also try my luck,' Prashant smiled and said.

'Best of luck Sahib,' Sub Babu said. They both smiled, and Prashant started walking towards his tent. Now he was worried about his family. The sun was setting, and clouds were approaching from all sides of the valley. It would not doubt rain again that night.

'Come Prashant, have tea,' said Vikas who was watching T.V. 'who is there on duty?'

'Thank you, Sir, Babu Sahib, is there,' Prashant said. He took the tea and pulled up the chair and sat. They both started watching the T.V.

'Sir, how can we make a call?' Prashant asked.

'You can call through our 'Fauji exchange' (official landline telephone for the army). Why have you not called until now?' Vikas asked.

'No Sir, actually last time I had made a call from Gangtok and after that, no signal, so I did not call. How can we call from the exchange?'

'You ask for a private exchange. Actually, the army has this facility that has a private exchange also. It will connect you to a civilian number. But there is a problem,' Vikas said.

'What is that Sir?' Prashant asked.

'It gives you just three to five minutes to talk. Not more than that.'

'That is not an issue. I will just say that I am fine, that is it,' Prashant said in a depressed tone.

It had been more than seven months; he had not seen his parents. During his training period, he was in the habit of going home after every five months; though in the first year of his training it was a bit hard for him after that he got used to it. So, for six months, he did not feel like going home as it was in his practice, but now he had started feeling homesick. Though, it had not affected his way of duty but somewhere in the corner of his heart that feeling had started.

'Come and watch, the media is showing something on Yakusla.' Vikas said increasing the volume of T. V.

'India and China have recently developed border issues, and it does not seem they will be resolved so easily. Our sources have said that the tension between India and China is increasing which may result in war,' The newsreader read.

'Why are they showing Chinese bombardment drill and all those other things?' Prashant asked anxiously.

'At least after one month, the media has shown this issue. That means now Delhi is aware that something is going on somewhere in India, apart from cricket and movies,' Vikas said ignoring Prashant's question.

'Sir, but why they are showing these hostile photos and videos? It is nothing like that over here,' Prashant again asked.

'This is the ground reality you are talking about. Even America is not trying to restore peace in the subcontinent but this way news will not be sold and neither the people of our great nation nor the bureaucrats will give heed over this issue. So, let the media exaggerate.'

'Is there any news?' the CO asked as he entered the tent.

'Jai Hind Sir,' Vikas and Prashant rose up and said.

'Call Mohit and Uday,' the CO sat on the chair and started warming his hands over the stove that was kept in the tent.

'Roger Sir,' Vikas said and whispered in Prashant's ear: 'send someone to call Mohit and Uday and also Gautam to bring four cups of tea.'

'Sir, green tea or with milk,' Prashant asked to clarify.

'Green tea would be better,' Vikas said.

'Roger Sir.'

Prashant went and sent a boy to call Mohit and Uday, and returned to the tent.

'Jai Hind Sir,' Mohit and Uday said as they entered the tent.

'Come and settle down. There is something important I want to discuss with you all,' the CO said.

Everybody took out their pens and a notepad and started listening carefully.

'We have to maintain peace over here. It is a different sort of war which we are fighting right now. On the ground it may not seem like anything will happen but a little spark and it may lead to war. We have stopped the Chinese plan of action and think of it in a way that they have been challenged by its neighboring country. Therefore, China will definitely not sit quietly. The best thing for us that up until now we have handled the situation very well and still there is a lot of scopes to get the problem resolved by a peaceful talk between both the nations' diplomats. So, we cannot give them even a single hint of exaggeration. For that, I do not want unnecessary movement during the day apart from the rotation of duty and in every duty; an officer will be with them. This will give them a boost in their morale. I do not want our boys to talk to the Chinese soldiers standing in front of them. Who is the duty officer for now?'

'Sir, Prashant is there,' Vikas replied.

'Ok! So, Prashant do you understand what I have said right now.'

'Roger Sir,' Prashant said and went out of the tent.

'Sir is there any discussion about its solution. It has been one month now,' Uday asked.

'Until now there have been three flag meetings, and I do not see any positive outcome. Now everything depends upon the BRICS summit. That summit is ten days from now,' the CO replied.

'But sir, today this issue has come up in the media also,' Mohit said.

'Yes! That is why we are hoping that the BRICS summit will give us some results.'

"BRICS is the acronym for an association of five major emerging national economies: Brazil, Russia, India, China, and South Africa."

'But the P.M. is in Israel,' Uday said.

'It is NSA level meeting, and our NSA is quite a sensible and powerful chap. Let us wait and watch. Ok then, I will take your leave. Vikas just keep a check on duty, and whatsoever I have directed,' the CO got up and went to his tent.

'Roger Sir, Jai Hind Sir,' Vikas said.

'Jai Hind Sahib,' Gautam said from outside the tent.

'Who is there? Come in,' Mohit said.

All three settled down on the chairs and started watching T.V.

'Sahib Tea,' Gautam asked with four glasses of tea on his tray.

'Gautam your timing needs to be improved; the CO has left. Next time, keep a track, whenever the CO comes, just bring the tea,' Vikas said taking the tea.

'Sorry, Sahib. Next time I will take care,' Gautam apologized.

'Just take care, now smile,' Mohit said looking at his sad face. Gautam smiled back and went away.

'Sir, Prashant was asking for leave. If it is possible,' Mohit said.

'Why?' Vikas asked.

'Sir, this year he has not taken any leave and moreover there are some issues at his home,' Mohit said clarifying his statement.

'Ok, I will talk to him tomorrow. Mohit, please call Prashant. Let us have dinner.'

'Roger Sir,' Mohit said.

'Prashant, wake up, it is 1300hrs,' Mohit said.

'Sir, please let me sleep. I only got to bed early this morning. Last night it was the coldest night I have felt,' Prashant said keeping his head inside the sleeping bag.

'Were you there the whole night?' Mohit asked in amazement.

'Yes, Sir.'

'But why?'

'Sir, actually I was chatting with the boys,' Prashant said crawling out of his sleeping bag.

'Prashant, your bunker is too cold, why is it so?'

'Sir, please sit on the bed. I don't have a chair. Sir, as you can see these bunkers are made of hollow blocks, and last night it was raining so heavily that the rain started seeping through the three adjacent walls. Just this wall was a saving grace for me.'

'But this stove?'

'This stove is just a showcase. It is really very cold Sir.'

Mohit sat on the bed which was 6'x3'. It was like a bed in a train's compartment. The bunker was sited tactically for the weapons, but at that time it was Prashant's room.

'So, what did the boys say?'

'Sir, just normal, everybody was anxious about when will we be going back and when will everything be over?'

'So, how did you respond?'

'Many a time it felt like those were my own voices. It was just like the movies, where our own ghosts speak to us and ask questions.'

'What did you reply?' Mohit interrupted.

'I just said very soon. I told them that the BRICS summit would definitely give a result. And...' Prashant stopped.

'And?' Mohit asked.

'And even I want a result from the summit,' Prashant whispered.

'I have told Vikas Sir. He will talk to the CO regarding your leave. That is why I have come to call you for lunch. So now, get up and come for lunch.'

'Roger Sir. Just give me ten minutes. I will freshen up, and then I will be there,' Prashant suddenly got out of the sleeping bag and put on his shoes. The bunker was still cold, but he was not feeling any of it.

In Fauji's life, leave is something which can even bring him back from the grave. Leave is the most exciting thing in the chronology of Fauji's life and for Prashant, it is happening after seven months. He had already made plans, in his world of leave's dream he was meeting his friends, planning his trips and his sister was going to college. For him, he was already on leave; just his body needed to be transported.

'Come Prashant, sit, have lunch,' the CO said.

'Jai Hind Sir,' Prashant replied and took his plate. For the last fifteen days or so he was continuously on night duty and because of that, he had not had breakfast and lunch. He just took one chapatti and two pieces of chicken.

'Do you want to go on leave?' the CO asked when he saw Prashant had taken his plate and sat on a chair.

'Yes, Sir.'

'Anything serious?'

'Nothing serious, my sister will be getting admission to college, so, some money will be required, and that is why I want to go home,' Prashant said.

'Ok! Where is she taking admission?' the CO asked.

'She will be taking admission into a medical college,' Prashant replied.

'That is so nice. But will you mind if you don't go for a couple of days?'

Prashant didn't respond, but he could never learn the art of hiding his emotions. His face was clearly indicating his disappointment.

The CO saw his face and said 'don't worry I will send you after the BRICS summit. Will that be OK?' the CO asked.

Prashant calculated something in his mind and in a low tone said: 'it will be fine Sir.'

'Now, cheer up, have your meal. What did I say to you?' Vikas asked.

'A chicken should not be kept waiting,' Prashant said with a false smile and started eating his food.

'Ok then, I will meet you all in the evening after the conference. Jai Hind,' the CO said and went to his tent.

'Prashant it has been a long time since we have heard your flute. Please get your flute,' Mohit said.

'Now, don't tell me that he plays the flute as well,' Vikas said.

'Yes, Sir I do,' Prashant said.

'Then bring it.'

Prashant went and got his flute from his bunker.

'You know, people say that it is complicated to stay out of the network for even a single minute,' Vikas said.

'What do you mean Sir?' Mohit asked.

'I mean out of Facebook, WhatsApp, and YouTube, etc. It is challenging, look at us; it is more than two months and no Facebook. What do you say Prashant?'

'Really Sir, had we been civilians we could have posted #nonetwork, #missingmahfacebook, #difficulttimewithoutuh, #lifelessordinary and what else?'

'Don't forget #mahlifemahrule,' Mohit added. Everybody started laughing.

'Prashant, don't be so sad,' Vikas said.

'Sir, I am not,' Prashant said.

'I could easily see the disappointment on your face when the CO had postponed,' Vikas commented.

'Sir, I have never asked for leave, but this time it is essential, and I will be required at my home,' Prashant said.

'Don't worry, just a few days and after the BRICS you will definitely go,' Vikas said in assurance and hope.

'Sir, I think we all will go after the BRICS,' Uday said.

'Wow, so optimistic,' Vikas said.

'Sir, with your permission, Prashant play some tunes on the flute,' Mohit said.

'Oh, I apologize. Please, Prashant, play something,' Vikas said.

Prashant checked the flute and like an expert played few notes and then started playing songs. After sometime when he stopped, everybody clapped.

'Prashant you are such a rare talent. What do you say Sir?' Uday said.

'That's true. But I don't know why he is behaving like 'Mathura Das' of the border movie? Now cheer up and go and check duty.'

'Sir, I am Batman. My watch begins at night. I am going to sleep now,' Prashant said.

'So, who will be on duty in the day?'

'Mohit Sir, I may choose to become Superman or Spiderman. I will rise at night. Goodnight Sir,' Prashant said and went back towards his bunker.

'He is very emotional,' Mohit said.

'He shouldn't be in Fauj (the Army),' Vikas took the last drag of his cigarette and crushed the butt in the ashtray.

'Mohit, go to the standoff,' Vikas ordered.

'Roger Sir.'

'**B**abu Sahib, are you from Kalimpong?' Prashant asked.

The weather was fine. For the last two days, there was neither rain nor wind. Even though the weather at Yakusla had not been merciful, yet both the armies were still standing face to face.

'Yes, that is my hometown,' Sub Babu replied.

'Then what is the problem over there?'

'There is no problem, why Sahib?' Sub Babu asked.

'There is some protest going on because of which even tourism has been affected,' Prashant replied.

'Oh! That Gorkhaland issue, it is not a new thing; it has been going on for a long time,' Sub Babu said.

'But why is there a protest?'

'Sahib, actually The West Bengal C.M. has made Bengali the compulsory language,' Sub Babu answered.

'And that hurts the ego of Gorkhas,' Prashant added.

'Yes,' Sub Babu said.

'And what do you think?' Prashant asked.

'I don't think anything about this.'

'But since it is your home, you must have an opinion.'

'Sahib, I also didn't like the idea of forcing the language. Why force Bengali over Gorkha?' Sub Babu said.

'That means you will also oppose it if you go home,' Prashant asked.

'I will not be part of any organization, but yes, after retirement I will join the movement,' Sub Babu replied.

'Babu Sahib, according to you what should be the solution?' Prashant asked.

'Gorkhaland should be declared as a state, and then I think it will be easy,' Sub Babu thought and said.

'But I don't think so,' Prashant added.

'Sahib, you are not aware of the situation,' Sub Babu said.

'That's true, I know, but I think Kalingpong, Rhenock and other parts are a type of autonomous region. Is it true?'

'Yes, that is. But....'

'Wait! Let me finish. Your movement is against language imposed on the students and your kids...yes or no?'

'Yes, but even if they want to impose Bengali then teachers should be Gorkha so that our people get employment and not Bengalis in our schools,' Sub Babu said.

'I agree with you. But what will happen if your children learn Bengali? Will they forget Gorkhali?' Prashant asked.

Sub Babu was not expecting this question. His mouth opened for an answer but without uttering a word, it automatically closed.

'Babu Sahib, I know your service is more than my age, but I will give you a suggestion if you allow me to,' Prashant said.

'Why not Sahib, you may be younger than my eldest son, but you are my officer, and I respect you. It is not just because of your rank but the maturity in your decisions. I would like to listen to it,' Sub Babu answered respectfully.

First time in his service somebody had praised him. The praise was not just mere 'flattery,' but that old man's voice had a seriousness and Prashant suddenly felt a heavy responsibility on his 'not so strong' shoulders.

'Babu Sahib, all these are the game of politics and power. Fauji's are very simple and ethical. Faujis can be fooled easily. It is just praise of our work, and we are ready to offer anything to anybody. Politics are beyond our understanding. See, because of this issue there are many losses. Schools are not being properly run, hospitals have also been closed, businessmen are facing the problem, and only politicians will benefit. A New state, a new district, new system and all new games of money,' Prashant said and paused and continued 'Sahib, there is no harm in learning a new language. Your child will know both the languages and will be beneficial for him in the future.'

'That's true Sahib. I agree with you. Even I was planning to go on leave, but when I had given a call to my wife, she also mentioned that vehicles and taxis are not being permitted in Kalingpong,' Sub Babu said.

'Sahib, we should thank God that we are in Fauj. These things do not affect us. Babu Sahib, you wait here, I will go and meet Wang,' Prashant said and started walking down the ridgeline to where Wang was staying.

'**N**i Hao,' Prashant said with a smile to a Chinese soldier who was standing just near the fence.

'Ni Hao,' The soldier replied.

'Where is captain Wang?' Prashant asked as he looked around.

The soldier did not reply. Prashant understood his plight. He tried very hard to explain. 'Where…Wang... Your boss.' he tried to communicate without words, only his hands were speaking. The soldier could not understand.

'Sahib, their condition is worse than ours,' Sep Ramesh, who was on duty there, said.

'Why do you say that, Raju?' Prashant asked.

'Because in India though we are not highly educated we understand a little English, but they can't even understand a little.'

'Yes, that's true.'

'And even their officers don't speak English,' Prashant nodded his head.

'Sir, you know standing in front of them even I feel more educated,' Raju said and started laughing. Prashant nodded in affirmation and saw Wang coming towards him.

'Hi, how are you? I was looking for you,' Prashant said shaking his hand.

'Namaste, Kaise Hai Aap?' captain Wang replied in Hindi.

'Wow, that's so good. Where did you learn?' Prashant asked in amazement.

'I am learning Hindi nowadays,' Wang said.

'Hindi is a straightforward language to learn. You will learn within a few months,' Prashant said.

'I hope so,' Wang replied.

'But Chinese is really very difficult. I am trying to learn, but I have been able to learn 'Ni Hau' only,' Prashant said.

'That's a good start, you will learn within a year,' Wang said, sarcastically.

'Leave it. Have your men changed?'

'Why?' Wang asked in confusion.

'Today, I see new faces. I had made a few friends with whom every day I used to talk in sign language, but today I don't see them. In fact, I guess everybody has changed,' Prashant said.

'Yes, that's true; our boss has decided to change the regiment,' Wang said.

'But why?'

'That's our policy. Within two to three months we rotate our men. So that everybody can get the exposure and even leave can be maintained,' Wang replied.

'That's wonderful, this helps in keeping them refreshed as well.'

'Yes, they don't get the feeling of boredom, but you have the concept of rotation of unit in two years if I am not wrong,' Wang asked.

'Yes, we don't rotate so early,' Prashant said, suddenly his heart started beating fast, and in his mind, he began going home, he looked upset.

'What happened?' Wang asked looking at his face.

'Nothing and why are you digging so much?' Prashant asked, changing the subject with a smile.

'Actually, we hate mountains,' Wang replied.

'What?' Prashant asked.

'Believe me, wherever we see mountains, we start making it flat,' Wang answered.

'We should not destroy this beautiful place.'

'For that, you must go back.' Wang said.

'You forced us to retaliate, otherwise; we are peace-loving,' Prashant took it personally.

'Let us not play the blame game. After twenty years when you will become chief of the army, then I will see.'

'Why, only me. We both will become generals, and then we will come for a flag meeting. We will begin trading, and we both will sit at this place in our chairs and will have beer and chicken,' Prashant had a sudden brightness in his eyes as he said this.

Wang looked into his eyes. Prashant was not joking. He knew that Prashant really wanted trade between India and China. He said: 'yes sure, we will open the silk route again. History will repeat itself. The golden era between China and India will flourish again.'

Suddenly a command echoed in the air, Wang turned left facing his flag. He stood stunned, and then at the next command, he saluted. It was a retreat ceremony. The Chinese flag which had seen more than one month of rain, wind and little sunshine was being wrapped, and all the Chinese soldiers were saluting. The retreat was for the Chinese, but there was a sense of respect even in the heart of Prashant. Though he would never salute that flag, he always ensured that during revile and retreat neither his boys nor himself would do any action that would hurt the Chinese sentiments. After the flag was brought down Wang turned towards Prashant and said: 'so Kabir, what will you do now?'

'I will go and watch the news then I will have dinner. And you?'

'Same here, now I have also accustomed myself to Indian timing. I guess, tomorrow is the BRICS summit.'

'Yes, let us hope of some diplomatic result.'

'Ok then, bye... See you.'

'Bye ...' Prashant waved his hands and turned back towards the tent. For him, the BRICS result was crucial because his leave was directly dependent upon it, and he was worried about his sister and parents. He was not only a soldier but was also a human being who had a mother and a father and had some family responsibilities as well. In this one month or so, he had been in a dilemma, and gradually this had started reflecting in his tone whenever he interacted with the other officers.

'What are your plans for Mohit's birthday?' Vikas asked putting his dinner plate down.

'Sir, the cake is not available and for liquor clearly 'no.' So we don't have many options left. Just as usual we will wish him a Happy Birthday, and that's it.' Prashant said finishing his piece of chicken.

'Sir, we will go to him at 1200 am and then wish him his birthday, but we have to do something else,' Uday said.

'It is up to you all. Mohit is your junior and Prashant's subordinate. So, decide and plan accordingly. This will be his most memorable birthday in the face of the enemy,' Vikas washed his hands and got into his sleeping bag.

Mohit was on duty at that time. It was one of the rare moments to see a clear sky when it was the full moon. The whole plateau was lit up. Many times, Mohit felt that the moon was nearer to him and if given a thought it was right as well. From 14000 ft it was closer than his hometown which was in Mumbai. It was clearly at sea level.

'I am going to bed. Even this clear weather can't give us a bit of warmth,' Mohit said, cursing as he entered the tent.

'No problem Sir. I had my meal. I will go and stand,' Prashant said and went out. Before leaving he looked at Uday's eyes, and both of them exchanged some kind of message, and then he went out.

'Prashant hurry up, it's already 2350,' Uday said over the radio.

'Sir, just a minute, I will be there,' Prashant started walking towards Uday's tent.

'Hurry up, pick up these two boxes.'

'What is this sir?'

'Just come with me. We will go to Mohit's tent. What about your guitar?'

'I have already taken it.'

'Good and the camera?'

'Oh! That I am carrying with me.'

'Switch on the light,' Uday tent told Prashant as they entered Mohit's tent.

'Happy birthday to you, happy birthday to you,' Prashant started singing and playing his guitar.

Mohit woke up. It was a pleasant surprise.

'Mohit, get up and cut this cake,' Uday said.

'Wow, Sir cake. How did you manage?' Mohit said in surprise.

'But what about candle Sir,' Prashant asked.

'That's not an issue. Get the cigarette over here,' Uday took a cigarette and after lightening it placed in the center of the cake and said 'hurry up, cut the cake and blow out the cigarette.'

The cigarette was blown out, and the cake was cut. Uday started singing the birthday song, and Prashant clicked away with his camera. It was exceptional for Mohit. He never thought that his peers would feel so much for him.

'But Sir, how did you manage this cake,' Mohit asked.

'Uday Sir baked it,' Prashant said.

'But how? It's wonderful, I have never had such a cake,' Mohit said.

'Thanks for your praises,' Uday said biting into the piece of cake.

'Sir, but please share the recipe,' Prashant insisted.

'Even I don't know. I have tried it for the first time,' Uday said.

'From tomorrow I will also try. Please tell me the recipe,' Mohit said.

'Ok. I have used Bournvita, chocolate, and milkmaid. By mixing these items, I have made it. Tomorrow I will show you,' Uday explained.

'Definitely Sir, we need to learn. Thanks for making my birthday so special and memorable. I will never forget it,' Mohit said.

Prashant poured three different juices into three glasses and gave them to Mohit and Uday.

'In the name of Mohit Sir, Uday Sir's cake and the Chinese, cheers,' Prashant toasted.

'Cheers,' everybody took a sip.

'Wow, it's powerful. Mix it with water,' Mohit suggested.

'Sir, please don't comment. Only this much I could do. Don't worry, the moment we will go back from here. We will celebrate royally,' Prashant said.

'With a royal black label,' Uday interrupted.

'No Sir, I will have royal monk, old monk,' Prashant said.

Three of them took a sip and then Mohit said 'Sir now, bottom's up.'

'Sir, it's Mohit's birthday today,' Vikas said.

Though Vikas knew that Mohit's birthday was celebrated at 0001 am, but the CO was not invited. He even sensed that due to the present situation the CO might have forgotten. Therefore, the moment the CO entered the tent, the first thing Vikas did was to remind him of Mohit's birthday.

'Oh! I really forgot. Thanks to you for reminding me. Where is the birthday boy?' the CO asked.

'Sir, he has gone to check duty,' Uday said.

'Call him.'

'Roger Sir,' Uday said and went out to call.

'We will not be able to celebrate in a great manner. But we can manage a cake I guess,' the CO said switching on the TV.

'But sir, I don't know, how will we get a cake for him,' Vikas asked.

Vikas had already called Gautam and passed him instructions for getting tea.

'There is a small bakery nearby. Prashant will go and get it. Though it may not be a perfect cake, the plum cake would be available I guess,' the CO said.

'I will call Prashant, excuse me, Sir,' Vikas said and went to Prashant's bunker. By that time the CO was surfing channels on the TV.

'Prashant get up,' Vikas said shaking him. Vikas knew that he would not wake up just by his voice; force was required to break his inertia.

'Sir... Oh! Good morning Sir. How come, you are here? Please sit Sir,' Prashant said leaving his bed. He was in a state of shock when he saw Vikas in his bunker.

'The CO is calling you.'

'Me Sir, but I have not done anything. And you could have sent someone else to call, why have you come? Is everything fine?'

'Put on your shoes, and go to the CO. I have come to light a cigarette. You know he does not like cigarettes,' Vikas took out a cigarette and put it between his lips. He searched for a matchstick but couldn't find one.

'Do you have a matchstick? I have forgotten mine, on the table,' Vikas asked.

'Yes sir,' Prashant replied.

'But I didn't think you smoke,' Vikas was not sure.

'No Sir I don't,' Prashant said.

'Then why do you keep matchsticks?' Vikas asked.

'Sir, for Agarbatti, sometimes when I take my bath, I try to worship God, so I keep it,' Prashant said.

'But in your whole bunker I don't see any poster of God,' Vikas said lightening his cigarette.

'Sir, I actually don't believe in any form of idealism, or Mandir, Masjid (Temple and Mosque) and Church. Actually, I light Agarbatti because of the fragrance it leaves in this bunker. That is like a godly feeling,' Prashant explained the truth.

'O.K. leave this philosophy and rush to the CO, he must be waiting for you,' Vikas said hurriedly.

'Roger Sir and what about you?' Prashant asked.

'I will come after finishing this,' Vikas said pointing to the cigarette.

'O.K., Sir.'

Prashant went out of his bunker and reached the tent.

'Come Prashant, I have a task for you,' the CO said.

Mohit and Uday were already sitting in the tent and Vikas had also joined them after finishing the cigarette. Vikas sat on his bed. Gautam had given tea to the CO, and one cup of tea was left. He was confused as to whom should he offer the tea. Therefore, he was standing in between. Prashant looked in Vikas's direction and then asked 'Sir what is the task?'

'Take a vehicle and go to Chumthang and fetch the cake. Right now, it is 0900 AM, by lunchtime you should be back,' the CO said.

'Vikas just brief the cook about today's lunch,' the CO ordered.

'Roger Sir, I will do that,' Vikas said.

'Meet you all at lunch,' the CO put the cup on the table and went to the conference.

'Why are you standing here? Go…' Vikas said looking at Prashant.

'Sir, I am feeling sleepy still,' Prashant said.

'Prashant go and don't forget to carry your mobile. If you are lucky, you may get a signal. So, it's a good chance for you to talk,' Uday said.

'And inform your girlfriend that you are fine,' Vikas commented.

'I don't have a girlfriend. Therefore, I sleep carefree,' Prashant said and went out.

'Did he just speak the truth?' Vikas asked.

'I have never seen him talking to anyone apart from his parents, and I haven't seen any girl's photo on his mobile,' Mohit said.

'I hope he is a normal guy,' Vikas said.

'Why are you saying that, Sir?' Uday asked.

'He is so talented and doesn't have a girlfriend. It is bizarre,' Vikas said.

Prashant reciprocated the wishes of soldiers in between the tent and parking area.

'Sir, where do we have to go?' Sep Chettri asked. He was the driver of the vehicle.

'Chungthang, let's go.'

'But any reason Sir.'

'Chettri start the vehicle. 'Let's go, I want to sleep. My eyes are burning. Please don't ask so many questions,' Prashant said.

Prashant sat in the vehicle and Chettri started driving. To avoid sleeping on the passenger seat, Prashant had put his Bluetooth headphones on, and started listening to songs.

'Sahib, the condition of the road is really pathetic,' Chettri said.

Prashant could not hear him, so he took out the bud from his right ear and asked 'sorry I couldn't hear. Can you please repeat?'

Chettri repeated his statement again.

Prashant said 'yes, that is true. The Chinese have constructed such a beautiful track within a month. Have you seen it?'

'That's right Sahib, if our PM visits this place, he will definitely give it to the Chinese.'

'Why would he do that?' Prashant was shocked.

'At least the Chinese would make it a blacktop road.'

'Yes, that is true. Actually, we should give a contract to the Chinese to complete this road as well. What do you say? '

'I agree with you Sahib; by doing this at least, our roads will improve. But Sahib you did not answer my question,' Chettri asked.

'Which question?' Prashant asked.

'Why are we going?'

'Today is Mohit Sir's birthday, and we are going to check whether a cake is available or not,' Prashant explained.

'Oh, that's great. I will go and ask for a treat from Sahib,' Chettri said.

'Definitely, but first let's get a cake,' Prashant said.

Prashant put on the earbuds again and started listening to songs. After a drive of half an hour, they reached Chungthang. The bakery had just opened.

'Chettri, do one thing, take this money and get a cake. I will go and try my luck on the phone,' Prashant ordered.

'But Sahib, what size?' Chettri asked.

'Any size will do and don't forget to get candles as well if there are some available.'

'O.K. Sahib.'

Both of them got out of the vehicle. Chettri went to the bakery, and Prashant started climbing the next spur line to check the availability of network signals.

'Oh Lord Shiva, today I need your help. I have to call home, it's urgent. Please help me with this network stuff.' Prashant prayed and manually searched the network. It is said that God listens to a man's prayer once a day and that was Prashant's moment. He called his mother's number hoping to get connected on the first go itself. It rang, and after six rings his mother picked up.

'Hello,' his mother said.

'Maa, it's me,' Prashant said.

'Where are you? I have been trying to call you for the last three days. It is imperative. Thank God you have called,' Prashant's mom said.

'What is it about? Has Navya got into college?' Prashant asked.

'Yes, she got into the college. But there is a problem.'

'What is that?' Prashant asked.

'This weekend is the last day to pay the admission fees,' his mother said.

'How much are the fees?' Prashant asked.

'7, 00,000 INR needs to be deposited,' his mother replied.

Prashant paused for a moment; he started calculating the money in his account.

'Hello, beta, are you there?'

'Yes, I am. Don't worry that will be done. I will arrange for it. But where is Navya?' Prashant said.

'She has gone out with Papa,' his mother said.

'Congratulate her on behalf of me, I have asked about my leave. Within three days, I will be at home, and then I will submit the fee,' Prashant said hopefully.

'We were all worried about how she will get into college without the money. Now, as you are coming home everything will be alright,' his mother said.

'Don't worry Maa everything will be alright. I am coming home. O.K. now, I should go,' Prashant said.

'Take care beta,' his mother said.

'You too Maa and tell Navya to buy anything she wishes, as her gift from me. Bye Maa.'

Prashant's mother wished him luck.

'Sahib, they have started baking right now. It will take some more time,' Chettri said as he walked out of the bakery.

'Ok, we will wait. Have you brought your mobile?'

'Yes, Sir.' Chettri said.

'Then you can call home,' Prashant said.

'Oh! Definitely Sir,' Chettri said.

Chettri registered his network and went a little further to talk. He sat on a stone and started talking.

Prashant kept his phone in his pocket, looked around and again took out his phone. He started scrolling through his phone's contact list. After a few minutes, his finger stopped on a number. He looked at the sky and dialed the number. There was a long ring. He removed the phone from his ear and looking towards the other side lifted his thumb to press the red button, suddenly a voice said.

'Hello...'

Prashant again put the phone to his ear. The voice repeated 'Hello... Hello...'

'Nidhi,' Prashant spoke with a heavy breath.

'Yes, who is that?'

'It is me.'

'Who?'

'Sorry, it's Prashant,' Prashant's words fumbled.

'Hi Prashant, how are you?'

'I am good, yes; I am fine and what about you?'

'I am also fine. Where are you nowadays?'

'Don't you watch the news?' Prashant asked.

'What sort of question is that?' Nidhi commented.

'Just say yes or no.'

'No, I don't watch the news,' Nidhi said.

'Oh! That means you are not aware of the present situation in India,' Prashant said.

'What sort of situation. Everything is normal. I mean I have not heard anything to be worried about,' Nidhi said.

'Oh! I see. Where are you by the way?' Prashant felt very disappointed. He thought that by that time the Indians must have known about the India-China issue and anybody and everybody who knew Prashant would be worried. But apart from his parents, he was disappointed that people were not concerned. For him Nidhi was everyone, and if she was not affected, that means nobody thought about him.

'I am in Pune and fine over here. You have not told me where you are? It has been a long time since we last spoke,' Nidhi said.

'Thank God you remember that it's been a long time since we had talked. Nidhi it's about one year. By the way, I am in Sikkim,' Prashant said.

'Wow, you must be enjoying it there,' Nidhi asked.

'Yes, I enjoy a lot here. In fact, we all are enjoying it here,' Prashant controlled his anger because that was the worst question someone could have asked him at that time.

'I envy you. Your life is so good. You enjoy so much,' Nidhi said.

'Nidhi, I want to ask one thing.'

'Prashant not again, I told you earlier also, and because of this I had stopped talking to you,' Nidhi said.

'Will you cry at my funeral?'

'What?' Nidhi said in a heavy tone.

'You heard right,' Prashant continued.

'I thought you were going to propose to me again,' Nidhi said.

'No, I won't, when we finish talking, please search on Google; India – China border dispute 2017. It will give you a result. It will also show you the place, where I am right now. Now just give me the answer,' Prashant asked.

'I think you are drunk in the daytime itself,' Nidhi commented.

'Will you cry or not. I just want to know?' Prashant asked the same question again.

'Nothing of this sort is going to happen,' Nidhi said.

'That means you will not come to my funeral.'

'Prashant listen to me. Why do you speak such words? People think of living and enjoying, and you are asking me about your funeral,' Nidhi said in anger.

'Nidhi, I know our people don't care unless and until they personally face any problems. The way things are going on; it may lead to war, and if that happens then, my "coffin" will come home. That is why I just wanted to confirm,' Prashant said.

'I don't think there is going to be any war. I don't like this emotional blackmailing,' Nidhi said.

'Nidhi I am not lying.'

'If there is so much threat you can see, then instead of talking to me you should focus on your job,' Nidhi harshly said.

Prashant couldn't tolerate such an insult and said 'Nidhi, I love you, that is a different thing, but mind yourself. I am not doing a job. It is a service. There is a difference between job and service which you will never understand. Go and search in a dictionary. Living in a big city does not make you literate, go and read more. Secondly, I have never forced you to love me. I don't force my feelings upon anyone. You know what, actually you don't deserve me. I am crazy. You deserve someone who does a Job, not a Service.'

Before Nidhi could reply, Prashant threw his phone. Chettri saw Prashant throwing his phone. He ran to him and asked; 'what happened Sahib?'

'Is the cake still not ready?' Prashant asked angrily.

'I will check Sahib, your phone,' Chettri gave the phone and went to the bakery.

Prashant realized that he had hurt the wrong person. He saw his phone which was covered in scratches, and put it in his pocket and walked towards the vehicle.

'I am sorry, Chettri,' Prashant said.

'For what Sahib?'

'I have talked very rudely with you over there. Instead of saying thank you, I scolded you,' Prashant realized.

'I didn't mind it, Sahib, you are a nice man I know; there must be some problem, that is why you are angry. Otherwise, I know you never speak harshly to anyone,' Chettri said in a very soft tone.

Prashant felt like crying, but he held his tears and said 'enough of buttering; now drive, the CO must be waiting.'

'O.K. Sahib.'

The vehicle started back. Prashant went back into his memories where Nidhi was his classmate; he fell in love but couldn't propose. After school, Prashant went for training and lost contact with her. But after commissioning, he again searched for her, and they started talking on the phone. Apart from his parents, she was the only one about whom he cared. He loved her so much and one day proposed to her, she refused him and awarded him with the title of 'best friend.' But Prashant didn't like the new title and proposed to her again, but she again refused. She had fallen in love with somebody else, but Prashant accepted that too and vowed not to love anyone else. But Nidhi couldn't understand his feelings and thought him to be a 'psycho,' and in her last conversation she called him 'psycho.' After that Prashant didn't call. In the last year he had just talked to his parents on the phone and nobody else, but every day he used to pray for Nidhi. Even after throwing the phone, he couldn't curse her. He could never see her harmed in any way, and Nidhi could never understand Prashant.

The rain had become an integral part of the life of soldiers at Yakusla. The beauty of rain was, the both nation's troops had to suffer or live through it. The rain had a special effect on Prashant's life. Prashant and rain had a connection. Whenever Prashant used to feel gloomy, the clouds used to gather, and before his tears, the clouds would burst. But it was not true for vice-versa. It started drizzling when he broke the phone, and by the time he reached Yakusla with the cake, a storm had gathered.

'Jai Hind Sir,' Prashant entered the tent.

'Jai Hind, have you got the cake?' Vikas asked.

'Any task given to me gets completed,' Prashant said.

'What happened? Are you upset?' Vikas asked.

'Sir, I need to go home,' Prashant said.

'So, have you made a call to your home?'

'Yes Sir,' Prashant replied.

'So, what is it?' Vikas asked.

'Sir, this weekend is last day to pay the fees,' Prashant said.

'Oh! That's too early.'

'Sir, I have to leave; otherwise, I will not get home in time.'

'That's really urgent.'

'Sir, please talk to the CO,' Prashant said.

'Definitely, I will talk to him. Don't worry everything will be fine. He has assured that after the summit you can go,' Vikas said.

'That I know, that's why I am waiting for tomorrow,' Prashant said.

'Call Uday, he must be on duty. The CO will be coming and give this plum cake to the cook. He will decorate it, and then we will celebrate,' Vikas ordered.

'Sir, but we need to wake up the birthday boy,' Prashant said pointing at Mohit, who was in a deep sleep.

'Sir, is there any news?' Prashant asked. The CO had settled down and asked for food to be served.

'Oh! Nothing much, let's see what happens?'

'But Sir the PM is in Israel I guess,' Uday said.

'Yes, he is.'

'Then... The summit?'

'It is NSA's meeting, and our NSA is an influential and visionary man. His visit will definitely give a positive result,' the CO said.

'That is true Sir. It is more than a month, and the weather is becoming worse each day. Let's hope it gets over calmly.'

'Let's see tomorrow. But where is the birthday boy,' the CO enquired?

'Sir he is coming,' Vikas said.

Gautam brought the cake and placed it on the table.

'The cake looks really nice. This is the best cake and the best moment for Mohit,' the CO said looking at the cake.

'Yes Sir,' Mohit said.

'So, what are we waiting for? Mohit blow the candle out,' the CO ordered.

'Mohit blew the out the candle, and everybody started singing the birthday song.'

'Prashant where is the guitar?' The CO asked 'bring it so we can have some songs. At least we can enjoy it, even though we will miss the beer.'

'Sorry Sir, the guitar is untwined, and I don't know it's tuning,' Prashant replied.

Everybody was shocked by the way Prashant had replied. It was not the guitar which was untwined, but his tone that was totally untwined. There was a moment of silence. Vikas understood the situation and said 'excuse me, Sir, I would like to say something.'

Even the CO ignored and acted as if nothing had happened and said 'yes, what is it?'

'Sir, Prashant needs to go on leave,' Vikas said.

The CO said 'let's see, tomorrow I will decide. Let's have lunch.'

Prashant wanted to speak, but his voice got choked. He had never spoken against any order from his seniors and against the CO he could never think about.

'Yes Sir, let's have lunch,' Vikas said, with a severe look on his face. He looked at Prashant and then took his plate and started eating his lunch.

'Jai Hind Sahib,' Sub Babu knocked on the door of the bunker.

'Who is there?' Prashant asked removing his earphones. He was watching a movie on his laptop. It was just 2100 hrs. And he planned to go on duty after 2200hr. Duty by now had become a regular schedule.

'Sub Babu'

'Oh! Sahib, please come.'

'What is the matter?'

'Is there any serious problem?'

'What is more serious than China over here?' Prashant said sarcastically.

'Sir, Sep Sagar's father, has passed away.'

'What?' Prashant got up from his bed.

'Today in the evening, I got a call from our peace location.'

'Where is he now?' Prashant asked.

'On duty,' Sub Babu said.

'Did you inform him?' Prashant asked.

'No, I didn't inform him,' Sub Babu said.

'Let's not inform him. Tomorrow I will talk to the CO and will send him.'

'And one more thing,'

'What's that?'

'Sep Ramesh's mother is distraught,' Sub Babu informed.

'I guess, he is the only son.'

'Yes, sir.'

'O.K. Sahib, I will talk to the CO regarding both of them and hope that they both get to leave,' Prashant said.

'Jai Hind Sahib,' Sub Babu saluted and left the bunker. Prashant sat down, and he resumed the movie. Within a few seconds, he closed his laptop, put on his shoes and jacket and went out to check duty.

'Hi Sagar, how are you?' Prashant went to Sagar and asked.

'Sahib, super fine,' Sagar replied in his usual enthusiastic tone.

'That's what I like. Whenever I talk to you, I feel more energetic.'

'Thank you, Sahib,' Sagar said with a charming smile.

'How's everything at home?' Prashant asked.

'Fine, Sahib.'

'When did you last call your home?'

'It's more than 15 days.'

'Why, people are talking on that ridge?'

'Sahib, I had given a call and said my country needs me so I may not call you (parents). Don't worry about me,' Sagar said.

'Good, you are really an inspiration.' Prashant tapped him on the back and went away. He turned and then again asked 'where is Ramesh standing?'

'Sahib, he is standing near the flag.'

'O.K., thank you, take care.'

'Jai Hind, Sahib.'

Prashant started walking towards the flag. In between, he asked every individual about their well-being.

'Hi Ramesh,' Prashant said.

'Jai Hind Sahib,' Ramesh replied.

'Jai Hind, how are you?' The soldiers near him paved a way as Prashant stood next to Ramesh in front of the Chinese.

'I am good Sahib,' Ramesh said.

'Don't you smoke? Somebody told me that you smoke,' Prashant asked looking at the Chinese soldiers, who were smoking.

'I have given up smoking Sahib,' Ramesh said.

'When did this miracle take place?' Prashant couldn't believe it.

'Sahib, he threw his cigarette away when he saw you coming,' The soldier next to Ramesh said.

'Why?' Prashant asked.

'It is because you hate smoking,' Ramesh said in a low voice.

'So, I hate smoking, but today I am feeling cold, and I want to smoke. Do you have a cigarette?' Prashant asked.

'Really Sahib,'

'Light up the cigarette, that is an order,' Prashant said in a heavy voice. Ramesh took out two cigarettes and offered one to Prashant.

'No, we will share, and you will teach me smoking,' Prashant said.

'O.K. Sahib,' Ramesh was surprised by his behavior because Prashant was famous for not liking smokers.

'You know, we can't fire a bullet, that's an order from up above.' Prashant said dragging on his cigarette and offering it to Ramesh.

'Yes Sir,' Ramesh took the cigarette and said.

'Then how will we fight?' Prashant asked.

'We are standing, how will we fight without bullets?'

'I will tell you a way,' Prashant said.

'What is that Sahib?'

'Whenever they light a cigarette, we all will light, whenever they eat one chicken piece, we all will eat two chicken pieces. Understood?' Prashant said.

All soldiers standing there looked at Prashant and started laughing.

'Yes! Sahib that we can do,' Ramesh said.

'Good, at least in this way we will show them that we can do more than what they can do,' Prashant said.

'Sahib, you know, today I was chewing tobacco, and one of the Chinese soldiers asked me for tobacco.'

'Then what did you do?' Prashant asked.

'I gave him and then do you know what happened?'

'How will I know?' Prashant said.

'Oh! Sorry. He gulped it down all at once, and then he fainted,' Ramesh said.

'Really,' Prashant exclaimed. For him, it was a funny moment.

'That's true Sahib.'

'If they can't stand tobacco, how will they stand against one bullet?' Ramesh said.

'Good, have you talked to your parents?'

'Yes Sahib, today I have given them a call.'

'How is everything?'

'Sahib, my mother is serious.'

Prashant acted shocked 'your mother is serious. Why didn't you inform me?'

'Sahib, my father said that I am doing a remarkable job. My country needs me, more than my mother. So, I didn't say anything.'

'That's so great about your father. You are really great,' Prashant said.

'Sahib, tomorrow will be the BRICS summit, and everything will get back to normal. So, after that I will see my mother,' Ramesh said with hope.

'That's the spirit, I also hope for the same. Good,' Prashant tapped his back and started walking towards the other soldiers.

Prashant went into deep thought. It looked as if he was meditating. He could feel a soft breeze on his cheek, he could hear the breeze, and he could see the whole Yakusla plateau without light. He could recognize everybody. He was flying.

'Jai Hind Sahib,' are you alright?' Sub Babu said.

'Why? What happened?' Prashant asked.

'Sahib, you have been standing here for more than 30 minutes, and you are not responding to anyone,' Sub Babu said.

'Really,' Prashant said.

'We thought something had happened to you.'

Prashant noticed that the other soldiers were looking at him in doubt.

'Nothing has happened to me. I am fine. Thanks for your concern,' Prashant said and started walking.

'Is there any news?' The CO asked as he entered the tent.

'Jai Hind Sir, no news at all,' Vikas replied.

'I think the BRICS conference is still underway. I have received a radio message from the conference at 1300hrs.' the CO said.

'Maybe Sir, but there is nothing on the news channels, they are not showing anything,' Vikas said.

'India is busy with the Presidential election.'

'Yes Sir, let's see; who becomes our President.'

'President is just a ceremonial post. You see, he is considered the first person of the country, the supreme commander of all forces. But in reality...'

'He is just a puppet.'

'That's true; he is just a political puppet.'

'Sir, in my opinion, the President should be someone who has been retired from the army,' Vikas said.

'Why?' The CO asked.

'It is because at least we have some ethics, morals, and courage to take decisions.'

'That is what political leaders don't want. Your qualities are only good in cantonments. They want someone who can just sign the bills passed by the cabinet and nothing else,' the CO said.

'Everybody wants a tiger, but it should be toothless,' Vikas commented.

'Yes, that is absolutely true. Where are others? Let's have lunch and then I will go to the conference. Let's hope we find a solution,' the CO said.

'Roger Sir,' Vikas sent a few boys to call the remaining officers.

'Jai Hind Sir,' Uday and Mohit saluted and entered the tent.

'Come, have a seat, how is everything? I hope you all are talking to your home and girlfriends as well?' the CO asked.

'Sir, everything's fine,' Uday said.

'You know, even I went to that ridge. I was told that mobile network functions over there and as a matter of fact, to my surprise, the moment I reached, my mobile displayed full network. I talked for a good hour or so. I hope boys are utilizing it,' the CO said.

'Yes Sir, they are,' Mohit said.

'Where is Prashant?' the CO asked.

'Sir he is coming,' Uday said.

'You name the devil, and he arrives,' the CO looked towards the entrance of the tent and said.

'Jai Hind Sir,' Prashant said.

'Come, Prashant we were talking about you,' the CO said.

Prashant smiled and sat beside Mohit.

'Sir, any news?' Prashant asked.

'Nope...' Mohit replied.

'Then why did he call me? I have no need for lunch as such. I prefer to sleep,' Prashant complained.

Vikas directed a look at them, and both of them shut their mouths.

'Can you go to the previous channel?' The CO said suddenly when Vikas was surfing the channels.

'Yes Sir,' Vikas said and changed the channel.

'Wow, this is my dream,' the CO said.

'What is that Sir?'

'This fire show, I want to go and see.'

'What's so good about it Sir? Every year we have a fire show in Diwali,' Uday said in between.

'I am talking about America. America's fire show is world famous. Though it is costly, it is worth going. Once in a lifetime, I will definitely go,' the CO said.

'Sir, America is really a great country. I am not saying because of its dominance over everything but its people, they have a very high spirit to fight,' Vikas said.

'That's true. My brother in law lives in Florida, and he says the same. Since childhood, they are taught to respect their country and flag. It is taught in school.'

'And in our nation, we debate over 'Bharat Mata Ki Jai' we should utter it or not. It becomes a matter of great issue,' Vikas said.

'Russia is again a very different nation. Once Putin said, I guess I read it somewhere that whosoever lives in Russia is Russian, nothing else matters,' Uday said.

'You know Sir, all these great nations are great because they have fallen and risen again, be it Germany or any nation and I think that is because of ethnicity. In Russia, people are Russian, in Germany Germans.'

'And in Japan; Japanese. Had it been our nation, after two nuclear bombardments, we would have been fighting for a loaf of bread up until today,' Mohit also jumped into the discussion.

'That's true. In fact, amongst all, Japanese are the strongest race. You know at the end of Second World War when they were losing somewhere in the northeast against the British, they did not surrender; instead, they jumped into the river which was full of crocodiles. There are so many accounts of their bravery written you should read,' the CO said lighting his cigarette.

'Bureaucrats and bureaucracy will kill us someday. We may protect from the outside, but from within, a revolution is required,' Uday said.

'Control your revolution Uday, the Chinese need you more,' the CO said looking at the angry face of Uday. 'Leave your revolution. Where do you plan to go?'

'Sir, I want to do scuba diving in Australia,' Uday said.

'That is so nice. And Vikas, what about you,' the CO asked.

'Sir, for me India is sufficient. I love to be anywhere with my wife and daughter,' Vikas said.

'Sir, I want to go on a Euro Trip, attend concerts like Sunburn, DJ Guetta and all, that is life for me,' Mohit said.

'And Prashant what about you?' CO asked.

Prashant remained silent. He did not answer.

'Prashant, the CO is asking you something,' Vikas said.

Prashant looked into Vikas's eyes and said 'I want to go home.'

'That everybody wants Prashant, but someplace that you wish to explore?' the CO said.

'I have explored enough in life, and now I want to go home,' Prashant spoke in a harsh tone. Everybody was surprised to hear Prashant's tone.

'So, you want leave,' the CO asked, grasping the situation.

'Yes Sir, I want leave, and it's urgent.'

'Ok. Let me come back from the conference, and then I will tell you. Don't worry. Now let's have lunch,' the CO said.

'**S**ir, they are showing a load of shit but no news of Yakusla,' Prashant said desperately.

'Don't be so desperate. I am sure there will be positive news we will listen shortly,' Vikas said. He continued surfing channels. They had been watching the news channel for the past two hours and yet there was no news at all.

'NSA meeting has just concluded, and no positive response can be seen on any side.' The reporter reported.

'What does the news say? Is anything good?' Uday asked, suddenly waking up from his deep sleep.

'Just wait; there is no official statement,' Vikas said switching over to another news channel.

'The India and China standoff does not seem to be ending as expected. Though there is no official statement from India's NSA. Though there have been talks regarding trade, Mansarovar, Yatra and Yakusla are still under the lockdown.' The media reported.

'I will not get leave now,' Prashant murmured.

'You will get it. Don't worry, it is not war,' Uday said.

'Vikas get me the feedbacks regarding our support weapons,' the CO said as he entered the tent in a hurry. Everybody stood up and wished 'Jai Hind.'

'Settle down gentlemen, I will give you some tasks. I want you all to give me feedback as quickly as possible,' the CO continued.

'Sir, is everything fine?' Vikas asked.

'We failed at our political level. Right now, we have to strengthen, that's the order we have received,' the CO said.

'That's what the news channels are also showing.'

'Leave the news and channels. They don't know anything. They are one of the reasons for our talk's failure. Thank God there is no live telecast of this place; otherwise, we would have been at war by now.'

Nobody uttered a word.

'Uday from tonight, trenches will be dug, and it should be in stealth. I don't want to hear any digging or hammering sounds,' the CO ordered.

'Roger Sir.'

'Mohit, site the automatics and show me. Go on the ground and see the possible targets. More overtake the accurate range from LRF.'

'Roger Sir.'

'Prashant you have to be extra vigilant at night and notice all the changes in duty. It should be as detailed as possible,' the CO ordered.

'I want to go on leave.'

Everybody's pen dropped, and eyes suddenly fixed on Prashant.

'Bastard, what the f*ck are you saying,' the CO burst out.

Prashant shook a bit but repeated: 'I want to go home.'

'How can you talk so cowardly?' the CO said.

'I am not talking cowardly.'

'Then how can you talk about going home. This is a war situation,' the CO said.

'It is not a war situation. Had it been war it would have been declared by the PM and since he has not declared war, I don't think by your opinion that it is going to be a war,' Prashant said.

'Prashant, move outside,' Vikas interfered.

'I will not go. I want a decision,' Prashant said.

'What will your company's boys think?' the CO asked.

'I will return if war is declared.'

'Do not act like a fool, what is so important that you have to go home? Your father can get the things done very well.'

'Whatever it is, that is my problem and since my father can't get it done that's why I am required,' Prashant explained the situation.

'For your sister's admission, money is required not you, I guess.'

'Then declare me dead. As such a dead elephant and a dead soldier are more valuable.'

'Have you lost your mind completely?' the CO asked.

'I have not lost my mind. You asked me whether I will be required or money and I told you the situation.'

'You speak one more word, and I will ruin your career,' the CO warned Prashant.

'I don't care about my career. I will serve until the date I want. Sir, according to me, you don't know how to manage.'

'Prashant, just get out,' Vikas tried to push Prashant out.

'Sir, just leave me. Let me speak. I am not afraid of any warning letters or any reprimands. I am not serving any person; I am serving this nation. But right now, my parents need me. He may get an officiating company commander, but my parents will never get any officiating son, my sister will not get any officiating brother. If war is declared I will come back I promise, but my parents need me right now,' Prashant's voice choked, and tears rolled down his cheeks.

'Prashant come, let's go out,' Mohit kept his arm around his shoulder and walked him out of the tent.

'Has he really lost his mind?' the CO asked looking outside after him. He felt a sense of rebellion, and that is the worst thing which can happen in organizations like the army.

'Sir, he is really under great mental pressure. His father has not received the salary from last two years, and because of this his sister had to drop out from college last year, and this year it's her last chance for medical college,' Vikas said.

'She can pursue B.Sc. it is also a good option,' the CO commented carelessly.

'Sir, if she wants to pursue medical college and if he is ready to take the burden of money, who are we to decide what his sister should do or not and even if we send him for five days, I don't think that anything is going to happen,' Vikas said.

'But there is no move order from the upper hierarchy.'

'But there must be some way. The day after next is the last day for her admission.'

'Ok, let me think then,' the CO thought for some time and then said 'if I manage the money and get it transferred to his father's account? I hope there will not be an issue then,' the CO said.

'I agree with you Sir, that is the most important thing right now.'

'Ok then, tell him to give his father's account number, and by tomorrow I will arrange for the money to be transferred. Tell him not to worry; his sister is our responsibility as well. In the heat of the moment, I said something to him. Just assure him that everything will be all right. Get me feedbacks. I will go and attend the conference again,' the CO said.

'Roger Sir,' Vikas said.

It was dusk. Prashant was looking at the Chinese tents. His eyes were full of tears. It did not matter to him that the boys were noticing his tears. For him what mattered was; his leave.

'Prashant you spoke so foolishly. From where did you gather that courage,' Vikas asked as he stood beside Prashant.

'I don't know Sir. I know that we are not supposed to speak out in front of our seniors. That is what we are taught, but I felt speaking as the best option at that time,' Prashant replied.

'That is what I like about you,' Vikas said.

'Are you not disappointed?' Prashant asked in surprise.

'I am, but you are so pure from the heart. That is the best quality of a leader. But…'

'But…'

'But you need to learn a lot. You can't be so direct and harsh. You have to be polite. That is a true gentleman. You are not only an officer of this great army but a gentleman as well, and you have to uphold it all. Isn't it taught in the academies?' Vikas asked.

'Yes Sir, it is taught, but it is complicated for me.'

'That is what you need to learn. I know you have an appetite for mythology and I have not read much, but in the Gita, Krishna preaches Arjun to fight himself before fighting others. Am I correct?' Vikas asked.

'Yes Sir,' Prashant replied.

'That's what the army is. Every day you have to fight with yourself, then only you can give a clear judgment, and you can lead your men. Merely passing out from the academy gives you the rank not the spirit of an officer. That spirit you need to develop. Men will follow you because they see your rank, but the day you prove your worth they will march till hell for you. You can't be weak on your home issues.'

Prashant wanted to intervene, but Vikas continued: 'I understand, you have a problem, but you are doing an excellent job with a noble heart, and God will definitely help you. Have faith.'

'Sir, I have faith, and you also know that there will not be any war,' Prashant said.

'That I know, but it is not peace also. Our enemy is standing eye to eye. In these situations, boys really need you for moral support, and the CO has assured that by tomorrow, he will arrange for the money. Just give him the account details,' Vikas said.

'Sir really, thank God,' Prashant's expression suddenly changed.

'We are family Prashant. You should remember that. That is the bonding we share in the army,' Vikas said and smiled.

'But Sir, apart from Sikkim, nobody cares about the standoff,' Prashant said.

'It is not like that,' Vikas commented.

'It is Sir, my friends don't know, Mohit Sir's friends don't know. Nobody knows apart from us, and for them, we are freezing our bones,' Prashant said.

'Prashant, take this letter and write a reply by tonight,' Vikas handed over a letter to Prashant and went back to his tent.

Prashant in surprise opened the letter and started reading:

"Jai Hind to all my Indian soldiers, on behalf of my school friends and neighborhoods I thank you all for standing there and saving us from aggression. I also wanted to be there and stand side by side, but I can't do as I have to study. I am in the 6th class and couldn't save much from my pocket money. But I am sending Rs. 2000/- from this year's pocket money. Thanks once again for making our lives safe and our future secure. Thank you and huge salute to all. Jai Hind."

Pragya Bharti,

From: Bangalore Public School.

Prashant's heart stopped for a moment. Tears rolled down his cheeks. A soft breeze started flapping the letter which he was held by both his hands.

'Who is there on duty?' Someone asked.

'I am here, don't worry,' Prashant replied and hauled out and started asking about the well-being of his troops with his usual broad smile.

-------THE END-------

Thanks for reading.

Your feedback is important.

Please share your valuable feedback and suggestion. You can reach us at girje.publisher@gmail.com

Visit our website: www.girjepublisher.com

Facebook: https://www.facebook.com/girje.publisher/

LinkedIn: https://www.linkedin.com/company/girjepublisher/

YouTube: https://www.youtube.com/channel/UC2YhHfdRu1VB0HqeCw2nkjA

Powered by AG Technologies USA, LLC - www.agtechnologiesusa.com

www.ingramcontent.com/pod-product-compliance
Lightning Source LLC
LaVergne TN
LVHW091513170726

843492LV00001B/469